CONTENTS

7   HE WAS DRINKING AT THE AIRPORT BAR
    by GARY YOUNG

9   THE BEAUTIES OF DRINK: AN ESSAY
    by LEE K. ABBOTT

27 PAUL NEWMAN'S HOUSE
    by LOU FISHER

35 SEALS
    by MARK HIGGINS

45 LIBERTY
    by MATT OLIVER

57 APRIL AT THE GARDEN OF DELIGHT
    by HARLYN AIZLEY

73 NUMBERS GAME
    by MICHAEL PIAFSKY

83 SOMETIMES THE BONES ARE VERY BUSY
    by G.K. WUORI

97 HICCUP TRICKS
    by BRUCE TAYLOR

109 PALS
    by KARL ELDER

119 FIGHT NIGHT
    by ROBERT FLANAGAN

133   GLANTON GANG
   by LEE CAPPS

143   THE CASTLE
   by MOLLY HOEKSTRA

157   THE GUY WHO THOUGHT HE KNEW ME
   by M.O. WALSH

HE WAS DRINKING AT THE AIRPORT BAR

Gary Young

He was drinking in the airport bar, and I asked, are you coming or going? I have been there, he said, and I almost didn't get back. He said, the engines failed, and we seemed to be falling forever; I've never been so afraid. Then he took a sip of his drink, and rolled back his sleeve. He'd printed his name down the length of his arm, and below that he'd written, Honey, I love you. It's strange, he said, what goes through your mind at a time like that. I hope to God this washes off, he said. My wife just loves to worry.

THE BEAUTIES OF DRINK: AN ESSAY

Lee K. Abbott

This essay concerns intoxicating drink—arguably the misunderstood subject of our era—and starts with my first, when I was eleven. The occasion was a party with dual purposes: to celebrate my daddy's fiftieth birthday and, a week earlier, his latest hole-in-one at the Mimbres Valley Country Club—for which Allie Martin, the club pro, had given him a gallon of Johnnie Walker Red. In point of fact, the person who gave it to me was Mrs. Hal Thibodeaux, and what she said was this: "Scooter, what're you looking at?"

I was looking at booze, of course, those decanters and bottles and crystal pitchers my mother had set up in the den near Daddy's trophy case. It was near midnight, I suppose, and everybody was quite instinct (a word I picked up much later at UNM) with madness. Mr. Levisay, for example, had Mrs. Dalrhymple collapsed atop the ottoman, and from the patio you heard a Fats Molydore harangue about pissants and such mossback peckerwoods as were tending toward Congress that year, 1958.

"A.C.!" Mrs. Hal yelled for my daddy. "Should I give this boy something to drink, or what? He says he's thirsty."

I had been yanked out of sleep by noises which are elsewhere described as common to apocalypse. I heard the words "fernal" and "wayward," plus a commotion in regard to games of chance, then my daddy, A.C. Le Duc, appeared from a dark region in the direction of the utility room, his hair flyaway and naughty. He wobbled, held his hands toward heaven, then said to give his son any goddam thing he wanted. So, while Judge Cleve Pounds was dancing the Cleveland Chicken with Ruby, our housekeeper, Mrs. H. poured me what I now call three fingers of redeye.

"Well, squirt," she said, heaving her bosom for effect, "here's mud in your eye."

How nice it would be to report, dozens of years from the event itself, that drinking whiskey had an impact on me instantly profound and disruptive as war. It did not. Instead, my mouth stinging and hot, I sipped, sat on a cane barstool Mother had bought in Miami Beach, and, like a late-movie spy, kept to myself.

Across the way, a cocktail balanced on his forehead, Goonch Ilkin kept referring to himself as one slick hombre, while behind him E. Terry Long was shifting his watery eyeballs in and out of focus. In the living room, I could see Alberta Turner showing Dottie Hightower her garter belt; and behind them, slapped against the wall like Christ, stood Mr. Harvey Kennebrew, whose face had the stricken inflamed look of catastrophe. Beneath the music— which was Paul Whiteman and din itself—you heard voices, harsh as cigar smoke, on a thousand issues: Sherman Adams, the AFL-CIO and Elvis Presley, as well as opinions on where taxes ought to go (down), what ought to be done with Lucille Ball's red hair (burn it), and how to get rid of Chinese hordes and their evil ways (bomb 'em!).

It, this party, was what I know now as life itself—a dreamland of ghosts and emotions and willy-nilly ideas—and, fixed on my stool, I had one thought: Lord, I like this.

~

Everybody talks about the horrors, which are real enough, but not about drink's beauties. For one thing, time disappears. As I once said to the second of my wives, Darlene, "Without drink, you're at the mercy of minutes." We were in divorce court, I recall, within gavel-throwing range of Judge Pounds himself. "With it, you can be here one second, drink for a while, then wake up in another land, months apart from the person you were and the place he lived in." You could wake to discover, I said, that you had missed any of a million terrors—including pestilence, drought, blight or cosmic decline. Drink enough, and you could ease into another, mistier world, one composed around the soft depths of sleep.

For another thing, pain also disappears. Once, for example, on my way down here years ago to teach civics at the same high school (Deming, New Mexico) where I had learned much, as possessed by drunkenness as the woebegone are nowadays clutched by God, I flipped my VW off a highway overpass, flew eighty yards—a six-pack of Buckhorn whizzing about my ears like grenades—crashed and tumbled to a crunching stop, doors crushed, interior a blizzard of clutter and clothes. The first to approach me, I am told, were two Buckeye tourists, who

11

peeked in, saw the mess I was, and gasped (in a single voice, I like to think), "Lordy, will you look at that?"

I was upside down and facing backward, everything of substance—cracked window, horizon, earth itself—running west and out of sight. I felt nothing, neither welt nor bruise nor open wound; and a time later I spilled out of that vehicle and lay next to it like a puddle.

"Howdy," I said, "my name's Albert Le Duc, Junior, but everybody calls me Scooter. What's yours?"

Those good Ohioans stared at me as if seeing a nightmare come to life. The man, particularly, seemed ready to bolt. "What's the matter?" I said, and the woman, perhaps someone's mother, pointed: "Your ear."

Sure enough. What used to be ear was now a pulpy flap, no more sentient than dried fruit. I fingered it carefully, more stupefied than frightened, then asked the lady to sit down, here, next to me.

"What for?" she wondered.

I was looking at our vast desert sky and feeling right tolerant of those without it.

"Well," I began, "I'd like to put my head in your lap."

For a second, I was convinced she might spit or kick me a little; she said, "Why?"

I took a deep breath.

"Comfort," I confessed. "I'm about to pass out."

That fall I took up the business of pedagogy, wore my hair long to hide my hearing-hole, and undertook in earnest fashion my higher calling to drink.

~

What you should know, now that this is being written, is that I am thirty-seven years old, no more debt-free than the majority of my fellow citizens, a regular voter, father of two (by the first wife, Jo Ann), and currently a resident of the Hot Springs Hotel in the scrub-covered hills above Hatch, New Mexico. This is no hotel at all, really, but that place addicted Americans like Betty Ford and Elizabeth Taylor might visit were they more middle-class and not so camera-shy. I am here at my daddy's expense, in an effort, he said, to "dry the hell out," which means bland food, rigorous exercise and a Marine Corps approach to mental health. Mostly, my story is not one of high drama—me being that vulgar Protestant many are or aim for—but I will, as part of my therapy, show you the good that drink is and how, sometimes, it makes us a better tribe.

Once upon a time, for example, I had a student named Butch in my eleventh-grade World Modern History class. This was during Vietnam, and Butch was a *West Side Story* hooligan who couldn't wait to be eighteen and an Army Ranger so he could whip the bejesus out of those foreign revolutionaries we were seeing on the *Nightly News*. He was as you are doubtlessly picturing him: slumped, bitter, and artfully tattooed, as well as expert in auto mechanics and most disenchanted by the charms of the Enlightenment. The only times, in fact, I liked the dirtbag was when I was drunk and then only because I saw him—and all of us, for that matter—for what he was: scared, weak and dumb. On the day I remember particularly, he was in the back row, making spit wads or arm farts, intending to diddle Mary Lou Feeny beside him; he was not at all attentive to the story I was telling about Diderot, about monarchies which are displaced, and about what a low-life species we'd be without the genius of Monsieur Montaigne.

"Scooter Le Duc?" Butch said at last. "What the hell are you talking about?"

13

It was a moment common in many places these days: old guy versus menacing younger version of himself. I was drunk too, which helped.

"Butch," I said, "c'mon up here a second."

It was late afternoon, our sun epic as always, and I knew that in an hour or so I'd be home, saying hello to my wife Ellen. By eight, I'd be orphic; by ten, asleep in a beer-hall never-never land.

"Right on," Butch said, pulling himself out of a slouch to commence that rolling walk he was famous for: hip, slide, lurch, idle, slide anew.

"Ladies and gentlemen," I told the class, "what you see crawling through the aisle is a bona-fide, triple-A, government-approved asshole." You could see the effect immediately: I might have been naked and roiling astride the busty Mary Lou Feeny. "Billy Jo De Marco, also known as Butch, is what you might call your basic ignoramus."

He was puzzled, not at all pleased, and I tried to watch his fists and lecture at the same time.

"What we got here is an American teenage dingleberry who likes food he can eat with his hands." That classroom, I swear, was alive with fear; you could hear plain as gunfire, many adolescent glands at work. "But," I said, "he's gonna do us all a service soon, which is get cleaned up and be a hero." Butch was almost to me when I felt my last Coors kick in. "Of course, there is the outside chance that he might, uh, die." Saying that word in front of teenagers is like saying "pussy" in church. "And if he does, I want all of you to join me at his funeral and sob as you're inclined to."

When he reached me, I threw an arm around his shoulders, gave him a brotherly hug.

"That preacher, if he's the sort I imagine, is going to say some mighty unkind but true things. He's going to mention, for one, that Butch here was young and, as a young person, liable to slip any time into an outer, eternal darkness. Furthermore, he might say that ol' Butch was a virtually certifiable cretin. Maybe a nose picker too."

I could see smiles, especially a wet one from Mary Lou F.

"But I want everyone here to know"—doubtless they expected me to cold-cock that boy—"that I love this youngster and do intend, on the occasion of his death, to weep abundantly and pitch myself into a pit of cold depression."

A bell was clanging somewhere, and in another minute I'd have thirty more live ones in here to entertain.

"Butch," I said, "pucker up."

Whereupon, quick as a cat, I grabbed that boy by the cheeks and gave him a movie-worthy smooch—a gesture of affection impossible in an otherwise sober man.

~

Another anecdote before we come to the big finish we're here for.

This scene comes from what is ostensibly the blue-hearted half of drink and concerns riot and Little League baseball. When I was married (to Darlene, number two) but separated, I went out one August night to Perkins Park to watch my youngest, J. E., play a little center field. Clad in Bermuda shorts and a ragged Lobo T-shirt (my legs a shade of landlubber white), I found myself sitting on a lawn chair beyond the outfield fence, my company those vagrants I am in continual sympathy with: pot-smokers, criminals of the mild sort, the lonely.

It was a wine night, I remember, brisk winds, heat swept south to Mexico, the clouds wispy and miles high; and the conversation in the twilight addressed the usual: moral concerns among the feckless, a lively discussion about taxes and who went where in the olden days of major-league baseball. Then, almost from the first batter, a man in the stands behind home plate started hollering, his speech that bray reproduced in our funny pages as "%$&**#$%!" According to him, what was happening on the field (and in the entire world!) was no less than blankety-blank with, for good measure, some so-and-so thrown in.

The third time he spewed forth—billingsgate, it was—a light flashed on in my soaked forebrain and I felt the presence of that which stands for principle in a drunk: outrage. I considered the fellows beside me—whiskered and wistful, they were, mottled and morose—then said, "I came here to watch a game, what about you?" You could see the idea catch them like a club on the chin, and when my nine-year-old took the field again, I called, "Hey, J. E., who's that sapsucker yelling?"

It took a second or two for him to find me in the shadows beyond the light standard.

"Ah, crap, Daddy, he said, "that's Bobby Hover's old man."

That inning I heard bile and foment, both; by the fifth, the warmth was gone from my heart. You could see old man Hover up there, the meager mom-and-pop crowd having fled from him as it would from rabies. Standing or sitting, he waved and yattered and spit, once racing down to rattle the chicken-wire backstop like a zoo monkey. "Yamma-yamma!" is what he screeched. "Fug, fug, fug."

The next inning, I'd had enough.

"Boys," I said, "let's mash that dipstick."

I was as brave on my Gallo Brothers diet as Charlie Atlas was on his regimen of iron and sweaty exertion; and, righteous with anger, we nonpaying sorts clambered over the chain-link to head for the infield. Euphoric and motley a mob as that which went after royal French mucky-mucks in olden times, our number included a dropout named Spoon, an older gent we called the Senator, two redneck grits who'd been to La Tuna for stealing railroad ties and a guy who looked like cement on legs.

"Daddy?" J. E. said as we charged past. "What're you doing?"

I brought my troops to a jerky halt and, calm as Reverend Tippit is when he sends his devoted flock to perdition, told him, "J. E., we're going over there and rip that man's liver out."

We reached the screen as a group and, hooting and yelling, we tumbled over and crawled up the bleachers until I was wellnigh in Mr. Hover's lap. He was built like Bluto.

"Who the hell are you?" he said.

Around us, it was Xmas Eve, not even a mouse astir, and I felt as Hannibal must have when he and his beasts broke through the passes and found all of civilization lying meekly at his feet.

"Mr. Hover," I began, "may I introduce you to my colleagues." I pointed. Over there, I said, dressed in a gritty sweatshirt and in need of a shave, was Plague. Next to him, a being with dental problems, Venery. Behind him, and quick with a fist, Murrain. "These others," I said, "I'm sure you already know." They were, left to right, Sloth, Malice and Greed. "So what do you say?" I asked. "Are you gonna shut up or what?"

For a second his eyes looked like coal which had lain for ten million years in darkness. You could almost hear him thinking it over, his brain fractured and flat as a dry lake bed. Then he rose, fat man's belly a counterweight, and said that for all he cared I, and my confederates, could die.

"You're drunk," he said. "Get out of here."

At this point, each of us had a moment alone with himself: Hover, for his part, was convincing himself I wouldn't; I, for mine, was convinced I would. Hovering between us, as stark and painful as are all visions of our dreadfulness, was the picture of what, given the breed man is, we might become: a tussle of legs and arms, hissing and snorting and whaling on our respective stuffings. I considered our heavens: it was a night worthy of *The Little Prince*. I spoke, trying to shape my words to express a thousand things—love, seriousness, resolve, etc.

"Mr. Hover, sir, I am truly drunk, drunk enough to see the two of you, but what I saw and heard offended not only me but also them, these interested parents, our youth and—" I did not know, I admit, where this was going—"and, well, It."

He looked confused, suspicious. "It?"

Around us, the no-account crowd was shocked and aiming to sneak away; in the lights swarmed millions of insects. Yearning for another sip of wine, I sought a gesture to include us, our ballpark, our town, our nation, the whole widespread world.

"Yeah," I said. "It."

The light came to his eyes, left again.

"Oh," he said, "right."

~

What you have heard thus far is what my physician, Dr. Spellman, says is just quote tears, tears, tears unquote—the whole of it attending to the shared theme of booze. "Scooter," he suggested the other day, "why don't you tell them about what brought you here?" It was a good idea then, a better idea now, and so, folks, I ask you to hie with me to a Sunday morning less than two weeks ago when my daddy, who's aged but awfully damn spry, rang me up to say that he'd put a foursome together for that afternoon and did I care to play? I had one thought, which may have been unspeakable, and another

which brought to mind links play and Sabbath-
inspired fellowship.

"Shit, yes," I said. "What time you want me
there?"

Until one o'clock, our tee time, I drank Oso Negro,
which is wetback rum and potent as TNT, polished
my Spaldings to a high shine, and stood in the back
of my Olive Street duplex, whanging a bucket of
practice balls over Larry Aiken's house and onto the
parking lot of Fenton Riley's muffler shop. It felt
good, I tell you, to be out in the sunshine and wearing
an outfit you might find one day on Pinky Lee; I was
especially pleased to discover that, more often than
not, I could still whack the ball with some authority
and little grief.

"Gentlemen," I said when I arrived at the first
tee, "ain't life marvelous?"

Coots every one, they were as depressing a bunch
as I one day expect to find in hell.

"Scooter," Willie Newell muttered, "you drunk,
or just crazy?"

I let them look at me for a second—my plaid
slacks, my red NuTonics, my stained planter's
chapeau with pheasant feather in the hatband—
then said something about the bear and the woods,
the Pope and Catholicism.

"Let's play sport, boys," I hollered, and soon
enough we were at it, each industrious as an old-
fashioned bookkeeper.

By the fifth hole, and in accordance with our
nassau, I was fifteen dollars in debt. "Hold it," I
said at the top of Allie Martin's backswing, "let me
figure this out." I possessed a pencil and a piece of
paper and tried, while Mr. Hightower screamed at
me, to bring order to this business of money and
competition. "Okay," I said at last, minutes later,
"let's resume." (I have had the opportunity, you
should know, to see that paper since and what is on

19

it is a sentence perhaps ninety words long, which
begins in the arms of virtuous reason and ends,
after several asides and trips to the hinterlands, in
a heartening muddle of hope.)

At the turn—only a couple of holes before R. L.
Crum started throwing his clubs and Mr. Newell
started beating on my noggin—we went into the
clubhouse for a sandwich and beer. I hadn't been to
the club much in the last few years, so I hurried
about, in the bar and dining room, saying howdy. I
told George Dalrhymple how much I liked his new
Biscayne and could I drive it sometime, my old Ford
being nearly unusable now on account of disinterest
and weak credit. "I'll get the keys later," I said,
"thank you." I saw Mrs. Chubb Feeny, reminded her
how much I missed those spaghetti dinners we had
at their place when I was in junior high. I was
arranging for a loan from Dillon Ripley when my
daddy creeped up on my flank, clapped his horny
hand on my shoulder and, in a doom-filled whisper,
said I should get my heiny out to the tenth tee,
pronto.

It was on the twelfth hole, a par five whose tee
is set back in what passes for woods in this desert,
that R. L. Crum fell apart like a three-dollar tuxedo
and I was set upon. I had stroked a beaut and,
hearty as Santa Claus, I told R. L., when he settled
himself over his ball, to widen his stance a mite.
"Pull that hand over, too," I added. "You look
terrible." There was a sun worthy of Brother Homer
himself and birds tweeting in the distance, and I
just couldn't keep quiet. "Hold that head down, R.
L. I got great eyes." Drinking a Bloody Mary, I was
trying to make contact with the soul of sport, which
is perfection, and perhaps the soul of us as well.
"Bend over," I told him. "Take some spine out of it."

What passed was a silence as honest as death:
in slow motion I saw R. L. snatch that club back,

grit, and fly forward. The ball blasted away; then, in an arc agonizing to behold, it dived to the right, smack into the core of a thick, thorny mesquite bush.

"Damn," I grumbled. "Ain't that a bitch?"

Here it was that R. L. spitting like a pressure cooker and thrown over into the underhalf of his spirit, whirled his club around his gray head and flung it thither. I was dumbstruck. "Whoa, now," I said. But in two giant steps, that old man, sputtering and making inhuman noises, had emptied his bag and was hurling everything—clubs, balls, his umbrella, a towel—into the plant life. I felt something let go in me—a muscle or comparable fiber. This was fury indeed, the sort, if it ends in carnage or conflagration, you read about for weeks; yet what was opening in me, near the heart or companion vessel, was a great flood of kindness.

I looked around. Nobody was moving. My daddy, a Chesterfield between his teeth, was as stiff as a fence post, nothing in his eyes about what a horror this was. Nearby, Mr. Hightower was picking at his thumbnail and maybe muttering to himself. And Willie Newell, otherwise glorious in his orange sport clothes, had the abstract, hooded expression of a snake.

"Wait a jiffy here, R. L.," I said.

He was now jumping on the bag itself, his voice part growl, part shriek. I tapped him on the shoulder, lightly, and he whirled around.

"Jesus," I said.

His face, normally blank and indifferent as sand, was crawling, patches on his cheeks red as sunset; so I tackled him. "It's all right," I said. I held that little man as you would a hysterical toddler, and tried to reach him as my mother had many times tried to reach me in a tantrum: "It's no big deal." He smelled as all these codgers did—dusty and not a little fruity. Take the long view, I told him. What did golf, or anything, really matter? We were just ooze, anyway, smarter and able to move on our own. "Think about it this way," I said, informing him of the billions we were, skinny, slovenly, robust—all of us fat for a larger fire. I said a dozen words to him— glee, mirth, salvation, etc.—trying to invest in each the entire weight of my person. "R. L.," I whispered, "this ain't so foul." I encouraged him to think of all, besides this immediate disappointment, which had not claimed him. Slaughter, for instance. Assault. Earthquake. And, well, diphtheria.

To be true, he resisted, scratching and slapping at me, trying once to gnaw on my neck. "You ought to be ashamed," I said. From my high, drunken perch, I was seeing him as woefully sore-minded, a poor loser who runs home to stew and maybe take it out on his furniture. "You stop that, now," I ordered, shaking him as more than once my daddy had wobbled me. "Grow up, you hear? What are you anyways?" You could tell he was lost, adrift like a castaway in his own despair.

"Aaaarrrggghh," he was crying. "Eeeeffff."

Big as I am, I held tighter and was reminded of times, mostly drunk-wrought, when I felt the world fall together as neatly as a deck of well-shuffled cards. "Well," I said, "what is it now?" In his face, now less than an inch from mine, was textbook apoplexy: the bug eyes of a frog, flared nostrils, lips quivering in a frenzy. "Listen," I began, "I want you to do something." For a second—or a minute—I didn't know what I thought, only that, warmed by vodka, I was as prepared as ever for the certain light of truth. "You get ahold of yourself right now, you hear?" We were on the ground now, him rocking in my lap. I made recommendations: Maybe he ought to fornicate more, I said, perhaps take up with one hefty as Mrs. Hightower.

"Second," I said, "get up a little later, you ain't missing nothing."

He was keening, moving toward the humble in himself, his voice a sobbing infant's.

"Third," I said, "throw off these expectations you have. Be firm in the present moment."

I had more to offer, but there was darkness somewhere, and something, bitter with ferment, was seeking to pass from my innards upward.

Then Mr. Newell, strong as a gorilla, clobbered me.

~

Two and a half hours later, Daddy and Sheriff Chuck Gribble came to fetch me; and, I'll admit, I was ready for them. What I told Dr. Spellman was that, once Willie Newell started thrashing on me, my whole frame of reference creaked, teetered, fell over and I leaped up angrily.

"Okey-dokey, you old farts," I said, "the hell with you."

And I stormed off, my stride purposeful as that seen at track meets.

I went straight home, pitched open my front door and aimed for the icebox. In it was what I'd been living on: various pressed meats, processed cheese I couldn't toss out, greens to make my sleep easier, grape jelly I had a yen for, and liquor. My anger was largely gone; but what remained was a parched spot which needed drink as much as a bird needs song. I showered—no small achievement when you're barely upright and coherent as chaos—and changed into my finest outfit: undertaker's sport coat, the shiny wingtips of a banker, and a Juarez, Mexico, tie which suggested what women are here for on earth. At some level, I knew plans were being made in my behalf, and I intended to accept them as if

23

they were wealth itself. So, smelling of Jade East, I sat on the porch, a tumbler of vodka between my legs.

What I'm going to say now will probably make as little sense to you as it did to Daddy and Sheriff Chuck: in any case, what happened was this: sitting there, heavy-lidded and numb, I had a four-alarm, wide-awake vision—one without fanfare or related trumpet work from heaven. I saw, from my aluminum chair, a world of shimmering elements and dancing lights and, suspended in them like angels, all the people I had known: Mother, my daddy, my Aunt Dolly, uncles, kids I had been schooled with. I saw my wives—Ellen, Darlene, Jo Ann—and, in rank beside them, my children. I saw, too, as if from a seam in our universe which happened to be on Art Monge's property, a file of strangers, each dressed for the big event of their lives.

"Well, I'll be," I said, and there they were, butcher, baker, etc., all lugging instruments of the loftiest kind: lyre, harp, flute. It was a goddam fashion show, what it was: formal wear and diaphanous gowns, arch headgear and glittery dangling rocks.

A couple of times I looked around. "Hey, Art!" I yelled at my neighbor. "You see anything?"

He was cussing his lawn mower and saying what havoc he'd like to wreak in this orb.

"Look out in the street," I hollered, "tell me what's out there."

He shook his head the way cops do over infractions of the mindless sort, kicked his machine to life.

I shook myself good then, closed my eyes and had a moment with myself. Okay, I thought. Relax. Think. What is this but another sort of pink elephant? I counted, as if playing hide-and seek: one-Mississippi, two-Mississippi. I listened to my heart: lub-lub, lub-lub. I took a deep breath my mother says airs the brain, and returned to the real world.

"Scooter," I said, "when you open your eyes, ain't going to see nothing in the street but sticky asphalt and your beat-up Fairlane."

I popped open my eyes and, again, took in that tide of whosits and whatevers that was flowing from its world into mine.

"Holy moly!" I shouted. "Isn't this something?"

I was a poor man getting lucky; and, as I knew I would, I spotted other familiar faces. I saw Butch, now in the company of Mary Lou Feeny and a handful of grinning, pink offspring. I waved, they waved.

What was in me, in my very cockles, was that joy associated with triumph, an emotion dear enough to forgive that done without it. I saw, you should know, those Buckeyes, now loosened from their place in my past and moving in front of my door in a manner downright jaunty.

"Hail, Ohio!" I shouted.

"Hail, yourself," they said and were gone.

I took a drink. Light was everywhere now, being splashed about and showered like rain. I even saw Mr. Hover, his fury vanished, and saluted him as you would those heroes who march down your street. Important as a drum major, he was leading kids, and they were bound for a place more amusing than Knott's Berry Farm. And then, about the time my daddy and sheriff Chuck rolled up in the old man's Continental, I saw that person nearest to me: Me.

Indeed, I could see myself as clearly as I now see this wall or that lumpy bed I dream on. Yes, there I was, shining and most benevolent, a bottle of booze in both hands, and a smile our white man's Easter Bunny would be woozy for. "How-do," I called from the porch; and, fetching as love itself, that Albert Le Duc, Jr., gleaming in the sunlight held open his arms and bade me enter. That Scooter who was in the street was bosom and lap and cradle—all those things we are inclined to fall into;

25

and, in an instant, I struggled from my chair, as Daddy and his minion started up the walk, and exclaimed, "Virtue. Desire. Beauty. Splendor. Wisdom. Charity."

The words themselves were another wonder in this world, and as I uttered them—even as I tumbled face first into my father's arms—I saw them, like birds, rising, rising. And never coming back.

PAUL NEWMAN'S HOUSE

Lou Fisher

O'Toole's was empty except for a woman drinking vodka at the bar. Emil took first a deep breath, then the seat next to her. He never would have been in a place like this, let alone daring to move in close, but what good had come from prowling the aisles at Barnes & Noble, from tending the machines at the Laundromat, or even from mingling with the shoppers at the mall after work. There seemed only this left to pursue, the neighborhood bar in his sad new neighborhood.

"I'm Emil," he said.

Her laugh rattled the still air. "C'mon now. What kind of name is Emil?"

"Good enough for my grandfather," he told her.

"Yeah, I suppose." The woman shifted toward him, crossing her legs on the bar stool forcing the skirt high above one knee. Though the knee caught Emil's attention, he didn't want to dwell on it. So quickly up from there and past the sweater of small breasts he paused at a deep red mark on the bridge of the woman's nose and then came to the mess of brown hair, all heavy and dingy, like a mop wrung out of basement water. She said, "Your grandfather, he wasn't born here."

"Well, no," Emil admitted in a whisper.

He was glad when his scotch arrived. Such jerky kid stuff, being teased about a name—though, yes, it had gone on in medical school too. Now that he thought about it, how about his boss at the clinic, that pinch-nosed crumb, always calling him Emil instead of Doctor. And every time he was the least bit late with Susan's check, she would wail his name over the phone and make it sound like a bird dying.

Why was all that?

Meanwhile, the woman had wet her lips with vodka. In that more focused way she said, "People ought to change their names when they come to America, don't you think?" Then she turned aside, set down the glass, ran her forefinger around and around the rim. Her face, in profile, seemed thinner, the corner of her mouth etched with spidery lines that brought her closer to his age. Her chin was pointy, but not too pointy, and it gave her a determined look. "I'm clear," she added, still toying with the glass.

"Clear about what?" he wanted to know.

"Listen," she said. "Claire—not clear." She studied him, a sideways glance. And though a spark seemed to come to her expression, it wasn't enough to brighten the bar or even to compete with the dim Tiffany lamp above their heads.

"Do you play tennis?"

"Well, I'd like to, probably." He felt a rush of breath at the thought. To be darting around. Swinging at a ball. With someone. "You do, Claire? You're good at tennis?"

"Helps that I'm left-handed," she said, and Emil saw now that her drink stood next to his, with that closer hand formed into an imaginary grip on a racquet. "Lefties hit the ball with a different spin and it scoots the opposite way," she explained. "You should see." But even as he attempted to picture a ball's bounce, the tint of excitement drained from Claire's face and her chin became an arrowhead aimed at his throat. "You don't play."

"No, not really," he said.

Then he caught her looking at his chest, at the loose silver watch on his wrist, and he knew she'd not give him credit for any sport, and she was right. Last year, though, after Susan left, he took swimming lessons. Now he could float. He could also paddle across the YMCA pool the short ways, in the shallow end, if he pushed off hard with his legs.

He tried to sit up stronger and straighter, but on the stool the tendency was to lean in, for balance. Made him feel even shorter than he was. Through a long obvious silence he thought of leaving the bar. Mumbling goodnight. Just going.

But wait...that would be giving up, yet again, maybe from then on, maybe forever. During his second shave of the day, and right into his own doubtful eyes, Emil had promised himself a full try.

"So where do you work?" he asked the woman.

"I'm sorry," Claire replied in a mumble. "What?"

"I asked you where you worked."

There was again no answer. Instead she peered over her right shoulder as two gray-haired men whispered by and settled, or huddled, further down the bar, almost to the very end. The lanky bartender stood there too, just beyond them, wearing unframed half-glasses and reading a tabloid. The tables were still empty.

"God," she said finally, coming all the way around to refocus on Emil.

"That bad?"

Her stare went blank.

"Your job," he said.

"Oh, that. Well, sure it's bad. Hey, what job isn't? Listen, every day I take a million shitty numbers and type them into the computer." Claire showed him how, pianoing her fingertips across the bar. Her nails were cut short but slapped with thick red polish. "By afternoon the screen gets to my head," she continued. Glows in through my eyes, so awful and deep--even aspirin doesn't help." She gave him another sample of that rattling laugh. "Hey, what does the company care? They've got so many bookkeepers."

"Quit," Emil said.

"Quit my job?"

"Yes. Right." He hadn't yet told her that he was a podiatrist. In a clinic at the shopping mall. Lower level. He was never sure why people found that so secretly amusing, what they snickered at—was it the feet or the mall? Maybe if his patients would stop taking off their socks in the middle of the glass-walled reception room. Ought to be a sign posted there, he thought. At any rate, fungus toes, dry cracked heels, bunions, corns, deep-rooted regenerative warts...distasteful, if anything. How had he ever fallen in love with Susan after smelling her feet? Well, the camphor liniment, that had helped. "You should just quit," he advised the woman at the bar, "and find something you like better."

"As easy as that?"

"Why not? You do it, and it's done."

"Oh, yeah, sure, don't I wish." Claire licked her lips, spit air, and arranged herself more evenly on the bar stool. So, okay, he thought, the chin was pointy. But aside from that he saw her somewhat better now. And what's more, he found that across the short reachable distance she was returning his look, brushing a few strands of hair from in front of her eyes.

"Would you like another drink?" he asked.

"No."

"But yours is almost gone."

"Forget it." Claire sighed and lowered her eyes.

"Well, I just thought—"

"Look, Emil," she said metallically. "You don't try to buy me drinks, and I won't try to keep you here. Is that a fair deal?"

He nodded; but lately nothing seemed fair.

Susan, for example, wanted a new roof on the house she'd taken from him, and much more money by the month. She was considering a return to court. She thought a podiatrist was like a heart surgeon, even though she knew quite well the meager annoying salary at the clinic. She assumed he'd had a raise.

Dammit, he should have had a raise.

His hand felt clammy where it rested on the bar. He leaned over and blew on the bar top, and afterward moved his glass more toward Claire's. Should have picked a better place. With music. With little wooden bowls of pretzels or those mosaic boards under wedges of pink-and-white cheese. Straightening, he caught himself in a deep and heartfelt sigh. He was here, and he'd better do something about it because how many more nights alone could he endure? Even if it didn't last with Claire, to have someone to talk to, someone to care about...

"I install security alarms," he said finally.

'Yeah?" said Claire.

"You know, security alarms."

"Oh."

"Sure. We did Paul Newman's house."

She was looking past his head. Her eyes were resting on something there, maybe the door to the ladies' room. Maybe so. They'd been sitting for almost an hour. Anyway, he couldn't tell if she'd heard.

"Paul Newman's house," he said again.

Now Claire looked at him, directly, and finished her drink. "Big place?"

"Sure. You can imagine."

"Around here?"

"Yes." He nodded a couple of times, emphatically, as if that would make it true. And true it might be. Why not? He was even beginning to feel strength in his jaw, like an iron rod bent exactly to fit. "Yes," he went on, thus boosted, "but out in the country."

She returned a faint smile, for only a second before her mouth recovered its familiar thin straight line. Then, as he had expected, she slid from the bar stool and went off to the bathroom.

Waiting, he stared at his fingers.

Though the medical fees in the shopping mall were relatively cheap and often discounted, this afternoon the clinic had been no busier than the bar. And just as quiet. Actually, he couldn't recall any day he'd been burdened with patients; even Susan, still at his expense, rarely showed up. The more he worked there, the more he came to believe that people with foot problems preferred to be treated at fancy professional locations, like that stone-front building over by the lake. So Emil, stuck alone in his cubicle, pegged away at the daily crossword puzzle in between appointments. His boss didn't like him to roam the mall, especially not in the laundered white jacket with the clinic's name on the pocket; and the boss's niece, who was the receptionist, never offered to bring Emil anything, though he'd seen other doctors get coffee, M&Ms, lottery tickets, whatever they wanted. And besides all that, what even now made Emil's jaw go slack and flooded his mouth with saliva, was that someone—he'd like to know who—kept putting his time card way high in the rack.

"That was fast," he said when Claire returned.

She shrugged and settled on the stool. With her left hand she wiggled the last remaining ice cube, or what was left of it, around the bottom of the glass. After several such swirls, she stopped and gripped the glass with both hands. "Why doesn't he live in California?" she asked, head still down.

"Who?"

"Paul Newman," she said.

Emil gulped in silence until she finally turned and met his eyes. Then he just said, "I don't know," and the bar seemed to close in on him.

"Well, it's probably the crime," Claire observed, frowning. "Out there those people keep coming across the border in the middle of the night. Right through the barbed wire, over the desert, and with names a million times odder than Emil." She glanced at her empty, lipsticked glass. "So what time is it?"

"When?" he said.

"Now."

"Oh, must be close to eleven." By tilting his watch, Emil managed to bounce a little light off its face. "Look at that, Claire," he said, himself surprised. "It's five after."

"Five after eleven?"

"Yes."

"Well," she said, "maybe one more."

Emil didn't know what to make of it.

Still, he signaled the bartender and ordered himself another scotch, a vodka for Claire, and when the drinks arrived he paid for them with the folded ten-dollar bill he had set aside for tomorrow's breakfast and lunch. He lifted his glass, rich in aroma, bountifully layered with ice, ambered full to the rim. Left-handed, Claire lifted hers too—the resulting collision threw a wave of scotch onto the padded front edge of the bar. A second later the drippings hit his lap. He tried to think of something to say, and the confession snuck out of him while he was the other half focused on the sudden dampness of his pants.

"I'm really a podiatrist."

Claire tilted her head.

"I take care of people's feet," he explained. "But you're a tennis player, you've got good feet."

"Oh, no I don't. There are times..." What started as a little squint of pain turned into a grimace that made her let go of the glass to clench a fist, an anguished fist that went tap-tap-tap on a dry area of the bar. "God, Emil, what I go through."

Gently he reached over and stilled that hand, uncurled her red-polished fingers one by one, and when he found them each to be smoother, softer than he anticipated, he could only hope that her toes would feel the same. "I can help you," he said.

SEALS

Mark Higgins

My church is the Assembly of Lost Love. I play parish
priest behind the hard, shiny wood that doubles as
confessional and altar. I pace from one end to the
other, from dishwasher to waitress station; the
waitress station is my favorite spot. Or should I say
I have a favorite spot on the waitress. I am, of course,
still in love with her, Pamela, although she claims
our love is dead. In the middle of the altar is my
One, True, Noisy god, the Cash Register. But my
flock believes in many gods, gods who reign over
them in the form of sparkling bottles. A drinker's
mythology: the great God Smirnoff made love with
the two peasant girls Grapefruit and Cranberry thus
creating Seabreeze, lovely soother of the windpipe.
My church has incense and icons and even the
ritual of communion, during which Yours Truly
serves the pretzels and vodka as the body and blood.
I hear confessions hourly. Hymns play in the
background. We have our shiny artifacts upon the

altar, our symbols. I wear my robes and am aided by Blue Nuns, Frangelicas, Absoluts, and a lay person named Jack Daniels.

The name of the tavern is Seals.

Behind the bar, on the wall, is a portrait of our most supreme God, Cupid the Talking Seal.The creature sits proudly on a rock, huge round eyes staring into the soul of each and every penitent. It is rumored that Cupid the Talking Seal possesses powers of insight into prospects of passion. Indeed, many a couple goes to Cupid's pool at the city aquarium and stands before him, awaiting his blessing. No bark, no blessing. A quiet seal means a doomed relationship. So the myth goes.

Cupid's services are expensive—admission to the aquarium is $24, so the less fortunate settle for me. Today I'll be dispensing counsel and absolution to many love-lost souls. The prerequisite of the counselor, the wise man: to be as screwed up as one's clients.

"Bless me, Innkeep, for I have sinned. It has been two vodka and tonics since my last confession. Innkeep, these are my sins." Bursting with guilt, begging for redemption, Parishioner Number One is Lawrence Kennedy, an early-bird-gets-the-worm-in-the-tequila-bottle kind of guy who greets me at the thick oak door of the confessional. "This sin is worse than all the others. Innkeep, I have dreamed."

"Don't we all?" I ask him.

"Not of a woman," he admits.

"Oh."

"It's not what you're thinking."

"I was thinking of getting some ice from the freezer."

"I'm not, *that*, you know."

Out of the closet and into the confessional. "That doesn't bother me. What did you dream about?"

"A seal."

"A Navy SEAL?" A man in a uniform. What the hell.

"No. A real seal. Cupid the Talking Seal." He points to the portrait behind me. "Our seal. My seal."

"Oh."

Lawrence is in charge of maintenance at the Boston Aquarium. I guess that's one of the dangers of working late nights with someone of the opposite species.

"Last night I dreamed Cupid and I were dancing, in my bathtub."

"Dancing?"

He nods. "Is this symbolic?" He asks because he knows I was a literature major in college.

I think of an old saying about dancing: Vertical expression, horizontal desire.

"Could I have a problem?"

He could have several problems, yet I remain silent. Pamela, the waitress, walks toward me, places her tray down, asks for two Heinekens. I have often dreamed of dancing with her. In my bathtub. I smile at her. She smiles back politely, quickly departs when I give her the beers.

Lawrence persists. "You've never dreamed of a sss—?"

"Never."

"It isn't so bad, is it? At least a seal's a mammal. I know people who dream of amphibians. Land animals. Their mothers! And we weren't doing anything. We were, dancing. In the tub."

Rub a dub dub. I dispense wisdom—unto myself. "Judge lest not ye be judged. Don't point out the seal in thy brother's eye without first removing the waitress' ass from thy own."

"Is something wrong with me?"

I shrug.

"I *love* this seal. In the honorable way. I swear."

"You want another drink?" I ask.

He nods.

"I've always liked seals," I say, as I look for Pamela.

"You have?"

Sebastian, my 86-year-old incredible shrinking man, walks in. Lawrence buries his head. He thinks Sebastian is crazy. A month ago, when I became pastor of this church of lonely hearts, Sebastian appeared six feet tall. He is barely four feet now. His chin is level with the bar. By the end of the year I expect to see his two small hands clinging desperately to the ledge. What accounts for his shrinking? Sebastian claims that the ghost of his dead wife has been pushing him into his grave. "She wants me back," he says, "but I'm not in such a hurry."

He orders a Harvey's Bristol Cream. He will knock the drink over after three or four sips. "She did that," he'll say. I will pour him another, courtesy of the management. He wears a French painter's cap over his head, pulled down low to cover the great scabs that cover his bald scalp. "What happened?" I once asked him. "Did you fall?"

"No, no, it's nothing like that," he said of his scabs. "The ghost has long, sharp fingernails."

Lawrence calls me over, secretively. He looks at Sebastian, turns his back to him, hunches forward, and tells me, "I'm going to rescue him."

"Sebastian?"

"No. Cupid."

"What?"

"Cupid. From the aquarium. I'm gonna free him."

Maybe what Lawrence meant to say was, "I'm gonna free *me*."

"My dream, I think it was symbolic. The dance of life. My tub is the ocean, don't you get it? I have to return Cupid to the sea."

Sebastian's eyebrows raise.

I begin to hum "Under the Sea," theme song to
Little Mermaid.
"I need some help."
You do, you definitely do, I think. My silence
bothers him.
"What? What's wrong?"
I keep quiet.
Sebastian, who hears all, now comments: "I bet
if you took a poll, ten percent of the population is
attracted to seals."
Pamela's eyes are big browns, framed by thick,
dark lashes. When I asked her out last week, she
said no. Just no, without any explanation.
"I'm going to free my seal," Lawrence says,
slamming down his drink. "Any last words before I
go?"
For your penance you are to say three Hails
and two Ours, is what I want to say. Instead I say
this: "Good luck."

Pamela's boyfriend is an idiot. He grabs her
under the arm yesterday as she gets off work, sort
of half pushes her in the car. I want to do something,
say something, but Pamela would want none of that
rescuing business. She seems, sad. The next day
she's late but I don't say anything. I love the way
her elbows bend when she ties the apron behind
her back.
"Are you OK?" I ask.
"No."
"Can I do anything?"
"No." Then she gives me her order. "A
screwdriver, two vodka tonics, a Lite, a Molson's, a
Beck's, and a noose."
I look at her.
She looks back at me.

When Lawrence comes in early the next morning, he looks like a lost man, unshaven, disheveled, reeking of----

"Fish. I smell fish." Sebastian raises his nose above the bar and sniffs.

Lawrence waves Sebastian off, motions to me to follow him to the end of the bar, where he whispers, "I did it!"

"Did what?"

"Cupid. He's in my apartment."

"Sure, Lawrence."

"I'm serious," he says.

"You've been drinking too much," I say. "Go home, pal."

That night, after work, Pamela sits with me in a booth in back. She tells me all, about the asshole boyfriend, about her lousy life. The White Knight role has always appealed to me. I want to rescue her from the dark tower, put her on the back of my stallion, ram my lance through the throat of her evil captor. We drink late into the night. We go to my apartment, talk until 6 a.m. I think I ask her to marry me. Though drunk, she has the wherewithal to say no. She falls asleep on my couch.

The following morning all of us read about it in the newspaper. Alas, the aquarium's preeminent citizen, the Pundit of Passion, the Seal of Approval, Cupid the Talking Seal, has indeed been kidnapped.

The regulars stare wistfully at the huge framed picture of Cupid, who is nothing less than a prophet, a mammal of the cloth.

Sebastian's eyes grow large and wet. He swats at the hands, real or imagined, that press down upon his head.

Someone suggests that the seal was picked off by the Irish Mafia: "He didn't talk a lot but apparently he knew too much."

I suddenly become an animal rights activist. I call Lawrence on the telephone and ask him, "Where's the seal?"

"I got him!" he says deliriously. "In my bathtub."

So dreams really do come true—"Are you doing anything to him?" I ask.

"Of course not."

"Christ, Lawrence."

His whispering is barely audible now. "I need to get him to the ocean. I can't do it alone. I need your help."

Pamela sits in the middle of the front seat of his car. Lawrence is on the passenger side, by the window. He is babbling about how he sneaked the seal out of the aquarium, how he is keeping him in his mother's bathtub. "She's in Arizona, on vacation." We pull in front of his mother's place, a brownstone in the Beacon Hill area. When we walk into the apartment the reek of the sea—fish, blubber, kelp, salt—assaults our senses. There, in front of us, upon the shag carpet, lies the seal. Pamela moves closer to me. From fear, more than anything.

"See, I told ya," Lawrence says. He walks over to the seal and kisses it. Right on the lips, if seals have lips.

I am disgusted. Pamela looks to me. I look to her.

"Cupid talks to me," he says. "I think he loves me."

I'm appalled. I want to call the SPCA. Or the National Enquirer. I want Lawrence locked up for life. But then, he looks at us and smiles. "We must return to the sea. Create a new race, half man, half seal. You'll help us, won't you?"

I am thinking of two things. One is of an old science fiction movie called *Waterworld*, starring Kevin Costner as half-fish/half-man. The other is of making a citizen's arrest on the perverted bastard Lawrence.

"Cupid talks to me about lots of things. When I mention you two, he barks. A lot."

I look to Pamela. She looks at me. Lawrence is a madman.

"He barks only when love is real. The seal *knows* what love is all about." Lawrence looks longingly at the creature. "And now so do I."

Pamela is embarrassed.

"Go ahead, ask him, about you and that jerky boyfriend of yours, Pamela. Cupid knows."

She refuses to patronize Lawrence.

"I'll ask him, then. Cupid, is Pamela's boyfriend good for her?"

Cupid remains silent.

"See?"

"Let's get out of here," Pamela says to me.

Curiously enough, I want to stay.

"Wait!" Lawrence begs. "Ask him about you two. You, Jim, you Pamela. I knew it would be only a matter of time before you two got back together."

"I have to leave," she says.

"OK," I say. But something in me wants to ask the seal.

Pamela heads to the door. "I'm going," she says.

"Ask, Jim!" Lawrence demands.

I look at Pamela; I look at the seal. I want to ask, but it's just too damned stupid, ridiculous.

Pamela stops. She doesn't turn around, but at least she stops, under the transom to listen. Part of me feels she wants me to ask, but part of me feels if I ask she will lose all respect for me. I decide to keep quiet.

Pamela sits in the middle, beside me. Beside her is Lawrence, who is donning a wet suit, fins, mask, air tank, the works. He claims it is inevitable that mankind will return to the ocean. He will be the first. Well, not counting Kevin Costner in *Waterworld*. In the back seat lies the ever-patient Cupid.

We are all quiet as I back down the slipway. We open the rear door, and Cupid climbs out, jinks his way into the water. Lawrence shakes my hand, then Pamela's, and follows the seal into the sea. He wraps his arms around Cupid's back, inserts his snorkel into his mouth, and the two of them disappear into the murky waves.

I look down, feel Pamela slip her hand into mine. She glances at me and smiles. Somewhere, in the distance, beyond the bridge, we hear a bark. A dog? Perhaps. But in my mind, and I hope in Pamela's, it is the bark of a different kind.

LIBERTY

Matt Oliver

Glenn Wilson watched a cockroach and a gecko rise
from the floor to form a sort of teepee, grappling at
the apex, each seeking an advantage. The gecko
ducked low to gain leverage, but the mass of the
egg-sized sumo roach was too much. Glenn leaned
forward. "Come on, gecko." The gecko fell onto its
back beneath the wiggling legs of the roach. Glenn
stood and kicked the fighting creatures, knocking
the crustacean on its back, then stepped on it,
savoring the crunching as yellow goop oozed away
from the edges of his shoe.

He slapped a hundred Piso note on the table in
front of Bob Ramirez, who was balanced on the two
back legs of his chair, feet crossed on the table. Bob
made no move to pick up the money.

"You get too excited about this crap, Glenn.
They're only bugs."

"It's hot."

Glenn stretched his arms, and breathed in the smells of exhaust fumes from the jitneys humming up Miksaisai Boulevard mixed with the odor of Shit River. Their table was close to the street, on the open side of The Fur Trader Bar, but the air was still and heavy and wet. Outside, the street vendors set up for the evening throng; jitneys, their lights just beginning to pierce the dusk, moved through pedestrians and motor cycles without regard for lane markings. Lighting a smoke and staring at his silver Zippo—at the aircraft carrier etched under the words "V.S.S. Ranger"—Glenn wondered when Nellie and Margaret would walk in. "Chief Myrick tried to keep me on the ship. Said no liberty until I finished updating the training records."

Bob had started a game of tossing nuts into the clean ashtray on the next table over. "Screw him."

"I hate that son of a bitch. He treats me like a damn dog."

"He treats everyone like a damn dog." A peanut hit the ashtray and stayed. Bob raised a fist in the air.

Glenn motioned the bartender for another pitcher of mojo. The first one had not lifted the weight of one hundred and twenty-one consecutive days at sea. He had been ashore for three hours, but the ship wouldn't let go; it was like crawling out of a hole he'd been in for four months. His legs were stiff and he was almost afraid to relax. He sat a little hunched, despite the heat, and rapped his fingers on the table.

The mojo went down smooth, tasted like Kool-Aid, but he knew that when it hit, it hit as hard as a ball-peen hammer. Nobody knew for sure what was in mojo, something red, with several shots of different liquors. Some of the guys said it was the formaldehyde that got you so wasted. Whatever mojo was, Glenn hadn't been anywhere else in the world where they could make it. He set down his glass and pushed it away, looked at the empty glass for a minute, filled it, and took another drink.

The energy on the street increased and the blend of sounds from outside drifted into the bar. A group of men cheered and tossed Piso coins at a local and his trained monkey. The monkey crawled up a sailor's leg, all the way to his head, then jumped onto the head of the next sailor. The voices were broken by a jitney horn, screeching tires and someone cursing in Tagalog. "He drives like that dude that just about killed us last time," Bob said.

"You're the one who wanted him to beat the British squids back to town."

"He did too." Bob resumed his peanut tossing.

"Spent half the ride on two wheels. You should've given him more than five bucks."

"He was happy. Damn Limeys could drink."

Glenn gestured across Shit River, toward the corrugated aluminum houses set atop bent wooden stilts. Discarded car tires weighted down the roofs. "What do you suppose they do when the wind blows?"

"They've been there for years. They figure it out."

"Some things you never figure out. You live with them, but you never figure them out."

Bob shrugged, lit a smoke. "I wonder what's keeping the bitches."

Glenn wanted to say that Nellie and Margaret weren't bitches, but it felt strange to stand up for a hooker's reputation so he let it go. The girls always knew when the ships were coming in, even if the sailors did not. They would be there, but they were working girls, and they had to finish their work. *You don't pay no fine because you no shit number one,* *Nellie had told him.* Glenn liked being no shit number one to somebody.

The lights came on inside, and the bar girls began preparing for the night crowd. They left Glenn and

Bob alone. All the girls knew Nellie. *I kick ass on
stinky ho I catch her with my man.* Sailors arrived in
groups of three or four: Texans dressed in boots,
jeans, and cowboy hats even though it was a hundred
degrees and humid; Californians wearing baggie
shorts, Teva sandals and t-shirts; New Yorkers, who
put in their earrings as soon as they got off the
ship, argued with each other, loud—but it was the
Marines that caught Glenn's attention. Of all the
Americans they looked the most unnatural. They
creased their jeans, and even their civilian shirts
were military pressed. Their hair was cut close up
the sides and about half an inch stood up on top—
jarheads. They called the hookers "ma'am" and
never cussed in their presence. Worse was their
gung-ho attitude: if a marine was told to peel a
hundred pounds of potatoes, he did it believing that
by peeling those potatoes he was defending his
country. Never doubt, never question. He turned
away from them. "If Myrick walked in here right
now, I'd stomp his ass, like I did that cockroach."

Bob brought his chair down onto all four legs.
"Will you quit talking about Myrick?"

Glenn looked up and saw the girls walking
toward the table. He stood up and hugged Nellie
hard.

"You miss Nellie?"

"I always miss you."

"You give me shit. You miss me till you come
some port and find stinky ho."

"I don't want no stinky hos. Here." He handed
her a large bag of peanut M&Ms.

"Where's mine?" Margaret asked.

Bob reached out and pulled her close. "Aren't I
better than candy?"

Glenn took a small box out of a plastic bag and
handed it to Nellie. "It's for Max." The box held a

cheap Timex watch that he got on the ship for ten bucks.

"You get jewelry for my brother?"

"He asked me for it."

She put the watch in her purse.

Bob poured drinks for the girls. Margaret pulled her chair close to Bob's and rested her arm on his back. The angle allowed Glenn a good view of her cleavage. Her breasts pushed up against her tight shirt, short enough to reveal her navel. She was, at least outwardly, sexier than Nellie. Nellie slipped her hand into his. She wore no fingernail polish, but her nails were long and manicured; she wasn't wearing any makeup, although he had seen her in it before, and her shirt, while it displayed the shape of her breasts well, was buttoned to just below her neck and tucked into her jeans. She wore sneakers. But she had a way of touching and looking at him that kept him coming back.

The club was filling so Glenn walked up to the bar for more mojo. Two marines sat on the stools in front of him. They wore their dress uniform shoes so polished that the bar lights reflected off of them. One leaned out of the way and said, "Excuse me," when Glenn reached for the pitcher.

"Bullshit," he answered and brushed the marine with his shoulder as he backed away. The jarhead didn't have to be so damned polite. What kind of doofus wore his uniform shoes to a bar?

When he got back to the table, the band had set up and was playing Duran Duran's *Hungry Like a Wolf.* People were on the dance floor. Glenn filled the empty glasses. Bob raised his voice and continued telling the girls a story about a plane with failed landing gear.

"We had to put up the barricade, a long net stretched across the flight deck, so the pilot could lay the belly down and skid into it."

49

"How plier come down like that and not crash?" Margaret asked him.

"Pilot? He's got it easy. All he's got to do is bring it in straight. Me and Glenn were on the crash crew. That's the hard part. We had to jump on as soon as it stopped and get the pilot out before anything blew. So he comes in low—like this." He started his hand toward the table top, banking it like an F-14 approaching the flight deck. "Then he hit hard." Bob slammed his hand on the table, and the girls jumped back. "Sparks were flying everywhere and me and Glenn looked at each other and said, oh shit man we're going to get our asses blown off. We ran toward the cockpit and the fire crew kept hoses on the wings, because they're full of fuel fumes and if they don't keep them cool they blow up the plane and us too if we're on it. So we went in through all this steam and shit 'cause the water steams up when it hits the hot metal on the bird, but we got there and pulled the dude out. He was okay."

"And when we got back to the shop, after the crash," Glenn put in, "that asshole, Chief Myrick said, 'what do you expect, a medal or something? Get back to work.'"

"Man. Just shut up about Myrick. He's a punk."

Glenn hit the table. "He had no fucking right to talk like that. Son-of-a-bitch. We risked our lives saving that pilot."

"Myrick suck," Nellie said. "I see him, I cut his ass good."

Glenn had seen Nellie use her butterfly knife once, in the Barrio, to run off some local thugs.

Bob got up for the next pitcher of mojo, and Glenn started telling the girls about a friend who'd been flown off the ship and sent to Leavenworth.

"It was a tough break," he explained. "Hunter had worked about eighteen hours straight. The plane couldn't fly until he finished, so Chief told him to work until it was done and sleep later. Who sleeps with planes taking off and landing on your roof all night anyway? And Hunter was on Myrick's bad side."

Bob had returned and was filling the glasses from a fresh pitcher. "The whole ship's on Myrick's bad side."

"Yeah. But you know Hunter, he didn't take shit from anyone, not even Chief. He did pretty good work, but his attitude got him in trouble."

Nellie put her hand on Glenn's back. "I know sailor with bad attitude."

"So the division officer comes in and chews his ass good, I mean Hunter's, and I thought he was going to cry. It was too much for him, and Poe starts in on him like, 'oh poor baby.' Well Hunter just lit into the kid, punching him hard. Poe tries to run, but Hunter won't let up, and Poe runs out of the shop, and Hunter kicks the door, steel door, like a hatch, and the door slams, but Poe's hand is on the edge and he couldn't pull it away, and the door slams and cuts his damn finger off, his middle finger, between the knuckles."

"I never saw so much blood," Bob said. "It was weird. Dude just stood there staring at his finger going, 'ahhhh, ahhhh, ahhhh.' I got a rag and wrapped it around his hand, and you could see the bone just sticking up. Anyway, a guy from medical came up and used a pencil to pull his finger out of the crack where the door seals and they sewed it back on. Looked sick as hell."

Glenn looked down for a moment. "They took old Hunter off on the next helicopter, with cuffs on. It was his own fault, but Poe deserved to get his finger cut off. He's always acting stupid."

"He's mellowed out a little now though," Bob said.

"I know—brave guy afraid of spider," Nellie said.

"I am not."

"We at home and Glenn see spider. Kill that spider, he say."

"It was huge, bigger than a tarantula."

Nellie made a space in her fingers about the size of a quarter and held it up. "My mom, she no kill spider, bad luck, so I catch spider. At night big sailor say, you think any more spider in here?"

"How can a guy sleep with tarantulas crawling all over the house?"

Glenn volunteered to go up for the next round. He stood behind the marines again and waited. One was about Glenn's size, the other was a little taller, full of muscles. He wondered how hard he'd have to hit the big one to knock him off balance. He nudged the big jarhead hard and said, "Move the hell over, I need a drink." The marine looked him up and down, moved out of the way. Glenn snorted, grabbed the mojo and headed back to the table.

"You know what?" Glenn set the pitcher down. "It sucks that Hunter's in jail."

"It sucks that Poe got his finger cut off."

"You're right. And it sucks living on a damn ship."

"The whole Navy fucking sucks."

"It sucks that people have to live on Shit River. But most of all, the biggest suck, the mother of all sucks, is that that slimy-ass cockroach kicked the shit out of my gecko."

"Here's to geckos."

"Here's to life sucks."

"Life sucks."

Glenn kissed Nellie.

"Maybe I won't go back to the ship. Maybe I'll stay here with Nellie."

"You stay with me and do what, clean house?"

He knew she didn't like it when he made jokes about staying. He might have loved her if the situation was different, but it wasn't. It was just the way things were. You don't marry a Filipino hooker. There wasn't anything Glenn could do about that. The other guys on the ship would never let him hear the end of it. It'd become a story.

Bob began another story. "You remember when half the ship got food poisoning from that chow hall corned beef?"

"Oh man, I never puked so much in my life."

"Oliver got it the worst. He turned green, I mean really green, like an iguana."

"That's what we call him now, Iguana."

"We all got it though, all of us on the night shift, and we had to go down to medical, but there was like a thousand guys down there and they didn't have room for us all, so they gave everybody an IV, and you had to hold the bag above your head with one hand and in the other hand you held a trash bag to puke in, but then you got diarrhea, so all these guys are running to the head with their IVs and puking everywhere. I just hung my IV bag on the coat hook in the stall." Glenn explained. "That way I could just sit there until it was all over."

Margaret waved her hand in front of her face. "Your ship stinky." Glenn lit a smoke and looked at his lighter. She was right, that ship did stink, the Navy stunk. He leaned back in his chair, examined the jarheads at the bar and thought that all marines must be idiots. A person would have to have brain damage to love the military so damn much. They'd probably all end up like Myrick: dumb-ass-lifer-dogs. They had to be stupid, and if someone didn't straighten them out now they'd end up ruining their own lives and hurting a lot of good kids. It was almost a sailor's duty to hit marines. He leaned close to Bob. "See that big jarhead at the bar? I think I can take him."

"Why?"

"Every time I go up for drinks he acts like a jerk."

"Shut up."

Somebody had to do it. Somebody had to put that big marine in his place. He watched them at the bar and took another drag of his cigarette. If he punched the big one hard enough, he could knock him off balance. That's all it would take. Once he started to wobble, it would be time to go in for the kill.

Nellie pulled Glenn's arm. "Come on, dance."

They moved onto the crowded and noisy floor and danced in a tight space in front of the band. They were playing "Wake Me Up Before You Go" by Wham, and it sounded pretty good, but it always seemed a little strange to Glenn to see a Filipino band playing American pop tunes. A slow song followed, and it felt nice to hold Nellie close. A sailor joined the band after that for "Great Balls of Fire." He was tolerable, and applauded for his effort. He'd be booed off the stage in the states, but in the Philippines you could do whatever you wanted. It was the land without consequences, most of the time. Other times the consequences were serious, like catching some kind of clap that made your dick swell up as big as an arm, or going to a jail where you got your ass kicked every day and slept with giant Philippine cockroaches crawling all over your ass. Once, a guy was killed by a mosquito bite.

Glenn was hot, so he took Nellie's hand and led her back to the table. Bob and Margaret were on the dance floor. He filled their glasses with mojo and took a drink.

"You having fun?" Nellie asked.

"Yeah."

"Forget about ship. You think about ship too much."

"I guess that's it."

He stubbed out his cigarette and walked up to the bar for more mojo. He stood, as usual, behind the jarheads. He reached out and tapped the big one on the shoulder. "Move over."

The marine stood up and faced him, "You got a problem?"

"I don't like you taking up so much space at the bar."

Glenn stepped in, pressing the jarhead closer to the bar. The ass was wearing his military belt buckle. His gig line was perfect. Anyone who looked that military off duty deserved to get hit.

He punched the marine hard in the face, but the jarhead didn't budge. Two quick counter punches knocked Glenn back. He caught his feet, went in again, running. The marine hit him and hit him and hit him, but Glenn kept coming. He got in close, reached out and grabbed the jarhead's throat. He felt the Adam's apple in his hand and squeezed. This was what he had wanted the gecko to do. The marine kept hitting and Glenn kept squeezing. He choked harder. The marine stopped hitting him and tried to pry Glenn's hands from his neck. Glenn clutched tighter and the jarhead started to fall back. Another fist found Glenn's face, and he landed on his back. He looked up and saw the second marine standing above him. The music had stopped. The bar was still. "We no want jarheads here," Nellie said, her knife straight in front of her. "This not jarhead bar."

The marine looked at her and smiled. "We can finish this outside."

"I don't have time for that shit," Glenn responded.

The large one had regained his composure, but Glenn could see bruises on his neck. That must be why they called them leathernecks, he thought, they were hard as hell to choke. Nellie's knife, not his fighting, had kept the marines at bay, but that didn't

55

matter now. Glenn stood. His right eye was swollen shut; his jaw hurt and the inside of his mouth was bleeding. That was okay too. He didn't have to be back on the ship for three days. He could stay at Nellie's until then, so he wouldn't look so bad when the other guys saw him.

"Shit. I was right there too," Bob said. "If the other one would've kept on, I'd have kicked butt. Damn. You just kicked the shit out of that big marine."

"It was nothing," Glenn said. He smiled at Nellie.

"You no need to be bigshot. You no need to act stupid."

She was a little upset right now, but she'd get over it. He filled his glass. "Sorry."

"It looked like he just jumped you for no reason," Bob said. "Damn jarheads, always think they're so tough. Two of them too, you took on two marines. You can't blame a guy for defending himself."

Glenn knew Bob wouldn't have been worth shit in a fight, but he was doing something now. He was making a story: the story about Glenn Wilson beating the hell out of two big-ass Marines. He leaned back in his chair and sipped his mojo slowly, letting it cool his mouth, holding it there a while, making it last as long as possible.

APRIL AT THE GARDEN OF DELIGHT

Harlyn Aizley

April's finally renting Table Four at the Garden of Delight. Table Four is primo, hot, da bomb. It's between the bathroom and the bar, safely tucked away from the front door. Girls working Table Four make like a grand a night. April's had her eye on Table Four for months now, and tonight's the night. She slipped Mike the announcer an extra hundred bucks and it was hers.

April's five feet six, blonde by Coco, breasts by Dr. Dave. She's earned Table Four. She deserves it. After all she was the one who started the faux leopard vinyl/spandex thing that's the boys' favorite. Tonight she's adding a leather halter-top that pops with one swift ladylike flick of the wrist and tug to the ends of the perfect butterfly knot; taught to her in secret by Jeanie (pronounced "Genie," as in "Yes, master," by the boys) before she left for *Miss Saigon*. The tables are synchronized, so if you don't pop at just the right moment you're "tits behind." A girl can lose money that way. If you're not showing, the boys move some place where it is—even if that means Table Two by the door or Table One by the phone.

Tonight is not just any other night, even though, as usual, the music at the Garden is so heavy with bass and drums that the entire room, floors and walls, pulsate like a giant throbbing incubator in which the boys, fragile and disoriented, are being kept alive. It's like working on the cardiology unit or intensive care, all these boys with their thump thump thump, all the sweat and heat and bad breath. April's a nurse, a doctor, a chaplain, stopping every so often to make sure her patients are alive and well.

"My don't we look fine tonight," she offers with a smile. "Hello there. How's papa?"

Instead of opening up and saying, "Ah," they oblige her with a smile and a five or a ten which means stick around until I'm not afraid to be alone. Fifty bucks later, April's on her way to the next one.

But tonight is different because tonight Louis "the manager" is coming. April met him working the casino this afternoon. She was looking all over for the fat slob at the roulette table with the cowboy hat and the southern drawl so she could deliver the amaretto sour he so rudely had requested, "Honey, be a good girl and try to say 'amaretto sour' to the bartender cuz I'd just love one." But when April returned he was gone, so she offered it to lonely Louis playing the nickel slots, and it turned out he's some big-time manager from LA, so she slipped him her card when the change girls weren't looking and told him to come see her at the Garden, she'll see to it he's treated right. Louis took a long slow drag from his cigarette, as if he already was sizing her up for some part or another, chased it with a sip of the amaretto sour and said, "All right."

April knows not to start looking for him until after midnight. That's when the casino gets depressing for people playing the nickel slots. That's when the tables are brimming over with Texans and starlets and piles of yellow and red-checkered chips that mean someone's blowing more than a nickel jackpot on each hand. Time for any self-respecting, frugal, LA-type manager to move on. She figures him for married, sensible, into it to a point, never dipping into the kids' tuition fund or his wife's weekly allowance. That's who plays the nickel slots, them and the old ladies.

April's beaming and the girls can tell. In the ladies room she practices puckering into the mirror. She licks her smear-proof red lips, slow and deliberate, and whispers, "I bet you play football," to her own reflection.

"April's workin' it." It's Chavonne, all pretty in pink and doing the kiddie thing this evening.

"What are you putting out for, April? An 'A'?" Sherrie, the new girl, thinks all the girls are in school like her.

"Just somebody who knows something." That's code for he's mine. When you score on the outside, you own rights on the inside. April's telling without telling. The girls get it.

"Good luck, honey."

"Take it where you need to go, 'A'."

Tonight is April's and she's feeling lucky. Table Four, the girls behind her, even Mike seems to be on her side. He's looking like he might "call her hot," which means call her name when the place is packed because even when you rent you share, and tonight April's got to share Table Four with two other girls also paying. But still for the last six months it was Table Two split four ways and that does *not* pay the bills. Besides, April's sharing with Alicia and Candy, both professional girls who can draw. Mike takes care of them because they took care of Mike in another life April does not want to know about, she's just a triple-threat waiting for a break and that's different from being professional.

April makes the rounds, sashaying around the room checking out the crowd, biding her time until that magic moment when the music stops and Mike calls her name, "On Table Four, it's Aaa-pril." She crosses her fingers behind her back that Louis will walk in at just that moment, in time to see her take the stage, create a presence. She wants him to see how she can maintain character even while dancing in heels, how she can capture an audience. For a moment she laments not being able to sing for him, but brightens at the thought of slipping a few lines into his ear during the lap dance he most certainly will order or else she will just have to donate, free of charge, for the chance to show him some more of her stuff.

April steals another hopeful glance at the door. That's when she spots them. She cannot believe it. Wouldn't you know? Wouldn't it be just her luck, on this, the night of nights? A group of women, as in "wimmin," squinting in the dimly lit foyer as they dig deeply into denim pocket for the fifteen-dollar cover.

"Damn dykes," April says underneath her breath as they take one of two vacant booths across from Table Four.

The wimmin order drinks. April slinks by their booth pretending not to notice. The other girls give each other quick glances.

"Yes!" Sherrie, a lesbian herself, thinks this is great. "Sisters at two o'clock."

But April is bumming. She knows LA's take on actors who play gay. You're out before you've had a chance to get in. And even if she doesn't have to play to these girls, even if they don't creep nervously up to the table with their dollar bills crumpled in sweaty adventurous palms, even if they don't order a lap dance just to test her or worse yet! to give her a presumptuous break from the boys, they're still going to stare. And when Louis sees these dykes staring at her she's out, a girl's girl.

April scowls at the wimmin so they won't get any ideas, and one of them winks back. "Shit," April says a little too loud.

Chavonne is all over them. She slinks past careful to brush her breasts against the tall blonde standing now to remove her coat. The wimmin squeal in delight, and Chavonne soaks it up. She's thinking she can squeeze at least a hundred out of them which is less than the effort would pay at a booth of boys but so much easier because the wimmin are right, girls *are* a break.

April is in no mood for this at all. She takes it over to an old guy sitting alone by the bar, and sure enough he waves a twenty at her for a lap dance, and she's so grateful for the distraction she almost convinces him she's in love. He keeps slipping her five after five, which under ordinary circumstances would be just fine but tonight's the night and as much as April does not want to be playing dyke to a booth of wimmin when Louis walks in, she also does not want to be making it with Grandpa, thereby causing her ticket-out-of-here to be the sudden and unwitting host of a multitude of distressing images, like pedophilia and life behind bars.

April's thinking all of this as she rubs her breasts back and forth, back and forth, across Grandpa's face. He's putting tens now directly into her halter and panting. April offers him a view of the rear so she can check out the door one more time and sure enough who does she catch stepping into the throbbing din, but Louis himself, eyes darting around the room, bills flowing like wine into the hands of Darrell the doorman.

"Louis!" April's trying to finish with Grandpa as fast as she can despite the fact that the tens have now turned into twenties.

"Louis! Over here!"

Needless to say, Grandpa's perturbed that his lady has diverted her attention. He growls and makes a face like the cowardly lion as he puts a bill back into his pocket. The faucet is then officially off, and April is free to roam. She bolts past Linda, the hostess, who gives her a look of warning. There are strict rules of etiquette at the Garden, for girls as well as boys, and not shouting across the room during a lap dance is definitely high on the list.

April could care less. If all goes well tonight, she's off to bigger and better things; just like Jeanie who once had three agents at a time at her table before the offer came to join the Broadway tour. April shoves out of the way Marcy, who unknowingly has offered Louis a drink, and whispers, "Amaretto sour?" in a sultry voice because it's Louis, and it's like their own private joke.

Louis looks confused. "Scotch and soda," he says tersely, but April registers it as to the point, efficient, no time to waste.

"Of course," she says. What was she thinking? Only fat slobs at roulette tables drink amaretto sours. Louis had just been polite at the casino. This is an audition, business after all. Scotch and soda. She blushes.

Half of the wimmin have gathered now around Table Four and are hooting it up with Alicia who plays to them without bias, takes their bills one by one, without a blink of an eye. Boys across the room crane their necks, ignoring the bounty in front of them, just to get a glimpse of the girl-on-girl action. Louis, himself, turns ever so slightly to follow suit, and April leaps in to distract him, "You know what I think?" she shouts to be heard over the music.

"What?" Louis reluctantly returns from the Isle of Lesbos.

"I think that even though women believe they're doing something empowering by going to strip clubs, all they're really doing is ruining business for dancers and putting on another show for the boys." April smiles slightly so he won't think she's humorless.

Louis' look is so cold and bland that for one horrible, earth-shattering moment, April wonders if he even remembers who she is, or if he just has stumbled into the Garden this evening by chance.

"I'm April," she reminds him. "I met you—"

Louis holds up her card and cuts her off without returning the smile, "I know."

"Oh, good. I was just remarking that we, as performers, really have nothing to do with this phenomenon of women going to strip clubs. If it was up to me—"

Louis glances at his watch.

"I should be going up any minute now." April gives the sound booth a nervous look. "Just as soon as Mike calls my name."

Tops are off across the floor but, as usual, it's Table Four that's hopping. Alicia, with nothing to lose tonight but a few bucks, is whooping it up with the wimmin, smiling even, having a ball.

Not April. She's so pissed now she's steaming. She leads Louis to the last available booth near Table Four and quickly races off to order the scotch and soda from Nick the bartender, who smelling distress, prepares it diligently and meticulously, not taking his eyes off of her for a second.

"Faster, Nicky," April says, because every second counts.

Nick hands her the drink but refuses to let go until he's delivered his assessment, "Women make you nervous."

"They do not."

Nick releases the drink but keeps his eyes on April. "It's okay. A lot of the girls get weirded out when women come in."

"Well, *I* don't. What do I care if some girl wants to—"

"Pity you?"

"Fuck you."

April is *so* not in the mood for any of this. She takes the drink and swiftly deposits it into the hands of Louis, who has removed the jacket of his Armani suit and has his eyes fixed on the all-girl show.

"You dance?" he asks, eyes locked on Table Four.

"Do I dance?! Of course—"

Louis interrupts her again, with a slow indecipherable nod, in tune somehow to the scotch and soda or the beat of his own complex managerial processing system. April is about to give a verbal rendition of her resume when, four girls in perfect unison, stoop to gather their halters and the collection of bills that have blossomed like flowers at their feet.

"All right," Mike's voice is smooth and low, comforting and provocative. "It's the changing of the guard at the Garden of Delight. Next up, on Table One, is Mar-cee. On Table two, let's welcome Tan-ya. On Table Three, El-eese. And on Table Four, it's Aaa-pri1."

The music rises slowly like the tide. Waves pound against April's ankles. A salty mist envelops her. Wade in the water, Aaa-pril, it's here, the audition of a lifetime. She closes her eyes for just a second, to get into character.

April is hot. It's like she and Table Four knew each other in a former life. They move as one.

Together, they're riding. The wimmin gather; all of them. Louis couldn't find a seat if he wanted to. In order to play to him, April has to notice he's not there, which means stepping a quarter of an inch out from where she is, deep in the sea and riding.

It's not like April never tried the old fashioned route to fortune and fame. It's not like she never waited tables, baby sat, or walked dogs for a living so she could perform in "plays without pay" at night in the hope that somebody who was "someone" would notice, would walk in and change her life. She'd seen it happen, from credit card debt to your own personal assistant. LA is full of overnight wealth, if not overnight success. But a girl can only wait so long. And after an impromptu song and dance routine performed in the dog park off Mulholland for a very surprised industry executive landed her in a police cruiser desperately trying to convince two of LA's finest she was assertive maybe, but not insane, April wised up. Rather than wait for Hollywood to come to her, she would go to it, legally of course. So she packed her bags and moved to Vegas, landing for herself, in only three months, a table at the best club in town. The casino is like moonlighting, a way to afford a new car.

Louis has downed the scotch and soda and ordered another. Every so often he extends his neck to peek past the wimmin and get a view of April who for the last five minutes has had her hand on the end of that beautiful butterfly knot, threatening to put the evening into fifth gear. She's moving in time to the music, milking the drums and bass for her own pleasure, courting the synchronized masterful splendor of it all when Sherrie, wandering freely after a forty-five minute two hundred and fifty dollar lap dance with a European tourist, happens by.

"Rock on, sister!" Sherrie raises her fist to April, siren supreme in a sea of wimmin.

It's like being woken from a dream, only this time April is being woken into a nightmare. Her hand freezes mid-knot, her eyes widen. She sees nothing but wimmin, and then off in the distance, so far away as to be reachable only by phone or fax or Morse code, sits Louis, downing the second and apparently last of his two scotch and sodas as he reaches for the bill.

"Nook!" April screams so loud that Mike stops the music. Linda turns on the house lights. And all of the glazed over eyes at the Garden of Delight turn to watch April climb down from Table Four, part the wimmin with a gruff sweep of her hands as if pushing open the heavy curtains of a hotel window, stand before Louis and declare, "I am not a lesbian!"

One of the wimmin, a shorter darker version of April, rises from her chair and announces "Neither am I." Her compatriots grumble. From out of the dark recesses of the Garden a man's voice says, "Too bad."

"Louis," April goes over and grabs the wrist of Louis who is frozen mid-transaction, the unpaid bill in one hand, his wallet in the other, "This seat is for you." She pushes him into the chair left vacant by the woman and proclaims, "All right then. Mike! Music!"

There is an excruciating pause as Mike and Linda exchange disparaging glances. And then the music resumes. The lights dim. The girls know somehow to pick up where they left off and soon it's tops-off all around and a sigh of relief is shared by all of those at the Garden of Delight.

Except the wimmin. The wimmin are pissed. They huff and puff as they take their time gathering their belongings, "accidentally" bumping into Table Four and even Louis who has ordered another drink and is sitting smugly as if the entire night were a show being put on for him in particular, which in fact, it is.

But April is back in the saddle. If she even notices the wimmin's departure she's reveling, in it, taking credit for the ejection of what she presumes to be the only oddity of the evening. April is the brave leader of all women working for a living. She is both feminist and feminine. She's showing Louis what it's like to be a man, to have a beautiful woman fight for you and then take you in and swallow you whole. And she's providing this service free of charge because Louis doesn't once dip into his wallet or his pocket to produce a bill. They're beyond tipping. They're making history. When the music stops April lets him down gently, eases him slowly back from paradise to the Garden of Delight.

"Out of here!" Linda can barely get the words out of her mouth as April rushes past her on her way into the girls' dressing room to collect her things.

"That was cold." Sherrie is offended, deeply. "Those women had as much a right to be here as any man"

"Listen," April gasps as she peels leopard from her slender hips, out of breath from her performance and the excitement of an audition well done, "Those women are not here to support you, Sherrie. They're here to gawk, to pity you for having to strip to put yourself through school."

"I don't have to strip. I choose to strip."

"That's what I mean."

Louis is waiting outside with a cigarette and his Armani suit. He is checking his watch as April, dressed in jeans and a sweater, bounds for the last time through the doors of the Garden of Delight. She swings her small sports bag over her shoulder and asks, "So, what did you think?"

Louis inhales deeply on the cigarette, taking in April's new outfit. "I'm staying at the Treasure Island Hotel. You got a car?"

"Uh, yes I have a car." April's thinking it's late for a meeting but this is Vegas, the city that transcends artificial conventions of space and time. "Should I drive?"

"Yeah."

April tries to push out of her mind images of limousines and tasteful office suites where other aspiring actors bring you coffee as you discuss contracts and negotiate deals with more decimal places than names attached to them. But here she is, driving her new manager to a late night meeting at a casino. To distract herself with some better news she asks again, "I mean my dancing was a little weak. But I thought it went well under the circumstances," she rolls her eyes. "How about you?"

Louis replies by blowing smoke against the passenger side window.

"It's closed," says April. "Would you like me to open it?"

"No." Louis doodles in the steam his breath has created on the glass. "Your voice could use some work."

"My voice? No one's ever said that before, but sure, okay. I know voice teachers sometimes join tours to, you know, keep performers fresh."

Louis nods and gives her another of his long, slow cigarette drag assessments, before turning back to the window. April presses heavier on the gas, hoping to shave off as many minutes as possible from this part of their meeting.

At the hotel, Louis leads April through the casino to the guest elevators. "We could go to the bar," April suggests and he grimaces as if bars were the most distasteful of all places. "This is just business

I presume?" April takes a step back from the elevators to emphasize her stake in the question.

Louis looks perturbed, like what the hell could this girl possibly have in mind and asks her, "What else would it be?"

"I don't know. I'm so sorry," April's pushing the "up" button herself now. "Please forgive me."

Louis' room is a disaster area with clothes strewn about and piles of brochures and magazines and dirty underwear. April tries not to look, tries not to register the fact that this is hardly the place to sign a contract or negotiate a deal. She rearranges the room in her mind until she comes up with a plan to get them seated someplace other than the bed.

"I've got to use the bathroom," Louis says already closing the door behind him.

April takes the opportunity to begin her remodeling. She starts by grabbing a pile of brochures from a chair. They're glossy and heavy, flaunting pictures of large mahogany desks and tall metal file cabinets. She pauses to longingly take in the picture of a crisp office with its boundaries and rules and sun-filled windows suggestive of what these last few months she has been trying to convince herself need not necessarily be true; that real business is conducted during the day amid secretaries and fluorescent lighting. She feels her heart start to loosen from the tight grip of her optimism and sink. To anchor herself in reality, albeit an alternative and unusual one, April grabs hold of the business card stapled to the brochure's cover and reads, "Louis Elkin, Manager, Sunset Office Supplies." The toilet flushes.—

April's sweating and shaking and thinking thoughts that are making her sweat and shake even more. Her hands can barely keep the steering wheel steady. Her mind can barely map out the route home to her apartment. An office supply store manager.

How could she have been so stupid? It had taken all she had left in her just to slip out of the hotel room and get her car from the valet. Now she's got to get home. It's practically four in the morning, and this is all just too much. April thinks a cup of tea might help calm her nerves enough to drive, maybe an egg, food for the new day. She purposefully hadn't eaten since meeting Louis that afternoon so as to better fit into her new halter and now she's hypoglycemic, that must be it; because stranger things have happened before, her hopes most certainly have once or twice been irretrievably dashed.

She pulls into an all night diner to fuel up. And there they are again—the wimmin. Sitting three to a side at a large booth by the window. April is standing with her arm outstretched and pointed toward her car, the poise of an urban cowgirl locking up. Doop doop. As if it's too late to get back in the car, she stands watching the wimmin, observing the way they pour coffee out of a communal brown pot, how they dip their forks into each other's plates and smile at the waitress.

"Something wrong miss?" It's the driver of a stretch limousine, parked modestly off to the side of the parking lot. He's kicked back with a newspaper and coffee, one foot poking out of his open window.

"No." Despite her efforts, April has had it with men for the evening.

"Long night?" the driver asks.

"Yeah."

"For the girls too. They got into it with some homophobe at a strip club and then found out today's shoot was ruined, so they got to do it over again tomorrow. Decided just to stay up all night I guess. Shoot starts at six."

"Them?" April points to the wimmin.

"Yeah," the driver nods in the direction of the window, "My harem. I drive them all over LA. Now I'm driving them all over Nevada. They're great though. Industry ladies. Very powerful. My daughter should make so many movies...and so much money."

April is listening with one ear and yearning with the other.

Louis the manager of an office supply store. The condescending wimmin, big industry execs. How could she have been so far off base? How could her lucky day turn out to be so incredibly unlucky? April rests a disbelieving hand on her grumbling stomach and peeks inside the diner. A poster above the cash register reads, "Hang in there, baby!" Next to the coffee machine another suggests, "When life gives you lemons, make lemonade!"

That's it. Maybe this all was meant to be. Maybe it's still true that when April woke up this morning her guardian angel had in store for her a way out of stripping in Vegas, and Louis the manager was only a pawn in that plan, not an actual player. Maybe his cosmic role was simply to lead April to the wimmin.

April smooths down her sweater and fixes her hair. She'll tell them she was acting, that was a part she was rehearsing for some hideous homophobic play, that she films by day but stays in character all night—that is how dedicated she is— that women rule and would they all like to hear about the camaraderie between strippers. It's great material, all of it. That is why she does it, after all, for the material. Her stomach growls again, even louder.

"Better get yourself something to eat," the limo driver says.

"I think I'll do just that," April tells him.

A string of bells dangling from the diner's front door jingles loudly as April enters. It's music to her ears, an orchestra announcing her arrival, at long last, she's in place in the show of shows.

NUMBERS GAME

Michael Piafsky

I smell him before I see him, like a bear in rain,
something wild, like ferns.

"Here's the list of people who can't get caught
drinking in bars like this," he says. Gray eyes and a
scar across his jaw. His back hunches downward
under an invisible weight. One of his eye sockets is
sunken in but he pulls the look off anyway. Patsy
Cline comes onto the jukebox, and I feel something
low down inside of me shift. My body doing the voting
for me.

"Kindergarten teacher," he says.

"Shrink," he says.

"Airline pilot," I say, leaning in on my elbow.

"That's a gimme. Intuitive," he says. "Florists.
Ferris Wheel operators."

"Judges at the Westminster Dog show," I offer,
and he smiles.

"Golf pro."

"Valet to the Queen."

"Accountant."

"Mayor," I say, into it now, trying to think through the muddy liquid in my glass. "Broadway choreographer. Traveling Bible salesman."

"This is too easy," the list maker says, pretty much when I catch my rhythm. "Now, jobs where you can be here two o'clock on a Wednesday afternoon." His hand is rubbing up gently against the side of his glass, matting down the hair on his wrist. I'm thinking garage mechanic, professional bowler, repo man, lumberjack, prison guard, but as soon as I offer these his face goes cold. "Nobody who's ever been in here has a job," he says and heads out to a stool at the rear of the bar. Midway there he stops and turns to me. "Leastwise none they kept."

There's about twenty of us sitting there, regulars mostly, but that's by face only. No names. Not the kind of place you come to meet people. The problem is that you'd keep seeing them day after day. Come some place to disappear and you don't want to disappear from it too. You'd have to keep finding new places and think of all the work involved. Like a bird building a new nest. Of the regulars, I'm the only woman, practically speaking. Janice comes in later in the evenings wearing makeup and a sweater that must have been the style in the Forties. Four drinks and she'll sing "The White Cliffs of Dover." Five and the tears cut through the heavy makeup and leave residue down the front of her pale pink sweater. Everybody here falls off the tightrope every night.

Here's something else about Pete's saloon. Every seat is flush against a wall, the interior as open as a landing strip. Ask Pete why and he'd tell you that in fifteen years no one has left their back exposed. Ask about the bar itself, the people sitting towards it, and he'd point out the mirrors. "People on those stools, their eyes stay fixed on the mirrored backsplash," he says and a simple look away would tell us it's true, except by now we're so far into our own baby blues that we're remembering echoes from the caves, our mothers tucking us in, the feel of those lips against our necks.

Another thing about Pete's: that selfsame listmaker takes out a gun and puts it on the bar in front of him and some part of everyone in the bar hopes they'll be the one to get it in the back of the skull. Make eye contact with the house painter three seats over and exchange a tired smile: man, has this guy chosen the wrong bar.

Turns out he hasn't.

Pete doesn't move, just keeps flushing the bottom of the dirties with a rag only marginally cleaner. Flicks moisture with his wrist, his eyes focused on the listmaker. Against the wood the gun gleams blue and silver. Shocking to see something so beautiful in a place like this.

"Mister, there's eleven dollars in the till," Pete says, his voice level. "You tell me it's worth it."

The guy smiles, shakes his head. From this angle I can see what I couldn't earlier when he was up close. I guess Man's the only animal that doesn't know when he's going to die. "I'm looking for a little more than that," he says.

"You've come to the wrong place," Pete offers, and somewhere behind me someone laughs.

"No, I haven't," the man says softly. "You folks look just about right to me. People call me Birdie."

Pete doesn't bite at this, his head moves down and then back up.

"Here's the set-up," Birdie says. "Everyone in here empties their pockets. Keep your jewelry, anything sentimental. Put the cash down right in the middle of the bar. All of it." He pauses for a second and then looks up, "that eleven dollars too."

Nobody moves, waiting for him to make some kind of move. He picks up the gun, and I feel breath leaving my lungs. Here it comes, I think. He opens the cylinder, takes out a single bullet and clears the chamber. We all hear the click. "One bullet," he says. "Six chambers. Just over a fifteen percent chance that I blow my head off."

"You want to repeat yourself?" Pete asks, his hand still wiping at a glass that hasn't been this clean since he bought it.

"For three hundred dollars I pull the trigger and all of you can watch," he says and then he raises his eyes and meets mine through the smoky glass behind Pete's ears. "And this little lady is going to make sure everything's square."

And I find my head bobbing up and down, my hand already in my bra for the twenty I keep for a real bender.

Apparently I'm not the only one with a contingency plan because within minutes there's a stack of bills on the bar downright respectable. "One thing about a place like this," the guy says quietly, his hands taking apart the gun to its simplest parts. "People bring every dollar they have every night." He looks at a drunk who has cleaned himself out so thoroughly that his lining hangs inside out of his pocket. "How about you, Emmett Kelly? No mortgage?" The drunk blinks and feels for the edge of his stool.

While I count the money Birdie takes out a felt cloth and starts cleaning the pieces. He polishes each part, rinses the smallest ones in his mouth to make sure they're spotless. "There's something about a revolver," he says, his fingers fluttering like birds' wings. "The springs, the pins, even the hammer. All of these parts work in concert for a single action. I suppose any machine is like that, but with the revolver the purpose varies. Human subtleties. The machine that cans tuna, I mean ultimately we're all doing the same thing with the fish. But a revolver? I guess there's nuance to it."

"What's that thing?" I ask him, pointing to a long, thin tube.

"Base pin," he says, without looking up. His fingers slide two pieces together and twist slightly. I notice his wrists are thin and graceful. Womanly. "Machines have a way of seeking companionship," he says, "the kind of thing that makes you suspicious, if you've got a mind for that sort of thing. The machine for canning tuna necessitates a machine for opening the can. Even Frankenstein's monster went searching for a mate. That's the beauty of the revolver. It's a machine that demands no one, a true loner, one and done."

Sure I saw his wedding ring. First thing I look for, force of habit. Signs and symbols from a past life. Back when I cared.

"What about the bullet?" someone mutters and it takes a moment for my eyes to focus. Tell the truth I'd forgotten anyone else was there. "Hush," I say. "Listen."

"What's your story?" someone asks from the back of the bar, and Birdie looks at me still counting the money.

"How much?" he says.

"Three-fifty," I say, trying to keep the astonishment out of my voice.

"For three-fifty I do it," he says. "For three-fifty I'll sit where you want, sing a song, tell your fortune or kiss your lady. But three-fifty doesn't get my story."

Funny thing though, two beers and a smoker's cough'll get you mine.

"The trick is finding the right kind of bar," Birdie says and people start to move in closer. Stools pulled across the wood tear like fingers at the floorboards. We're packed in so close we can almost touch each other, all except Pete who's still behind the bar. I'm holding the money in my hands, rubbing the stack of bills against each other for their smell, something almost human coming up to my nostrils. Someone coughs.

Birdie starts talking again, almost to himself. Almost offhand. "Go to some other kind of place, a nicer one, of course I'd make more money but there'd be risks."

"Police," someone offers and Birdie looks up, as if surprised.

"Yeah, police, sure. But other things too. Wrong kind of bar and a gun is sort of an invitation."

"Yeah, you wouldn't want to try this in a sketchy place," we say, laughing.

Birdie acknowledges his surroundings and shrugs. "I'm only telling you what I know," he says. "Bar like this there's never a problem."

"What are the other risks?" I ask, and for a moment his eyes meet mine and I think, though I can't be sure, that he winks.

"Oh, all sorts of things," he says. "Someone comes to a bar with a date, this isn't the sort of thing they're hoping for. This ain't foreplay."

"Not for them anyway."

"No," he says. "No. Not for any of us. No." And for a second his entire face contorts and no one, not even the neediest junkie in the bar regrets his purchase.

"Besides," he says, his voice lightening. "Those meat markets uptown, blood on mirrors wouldn't go with their decor. There'd be cleaning costs. Speaking of which," he leans over to me, and I can feel his breath on my breasts, my body straining forward to meet it. He plucks a five from my fingers, crumples it and sails it over to Pete. This'll cover the sawdust," he says and Pete stuffs the bill into his pocket.

Then Birdie's hands punch the table, and we all spring back. He laughs, a cough that moves something in his lungs. "Sorry," he says. "Just about time to begin. Where do you want me?" He lifts the gun, and we see it put back together, its slim shape resurrected, the power and life, its pearl handle streamlined for our comfort, its bluing oil impatient.

We think for a moment and motion him into the back, against the outside wall. I want to ask if this is where they usually put him, if there is any consistency, but the question dies somewhere in my throat. He leans up easily against the sweating concrete rocks the small of his back up and down, a tomcat getting his bearings. He motions me forward, and the crowd splits in front of me. He hands me the gun, and I almost drop it for its weight. Then his fingers move me until everyone can see him clearly. He takes out a bullet and holds it up to the light. Whereas the gun looks functional, oiled, the bullet looks virginal. It is an arrow to the heavens, a sparrow in flight. High fucking art. He puts it into a chamber and motions for me to do the honors. I turn my back to him and raise the gun. When I spin, my fingers grazing the cylinder, my heart spins too, and when I lock the chamber in place I almost collapse from lightheadedness. We all, instinctively look back at him to see if he has tried to catch a glimpse of the lucky chamber. Grinning he places his hand above his eyes and then, still grinning, spreads his fingers wide.

By now, into it a little, I rotate my hips and start to hand the gun back to him with a flourish, the knife thrower's flamenco. He refuses it, holds up his hand and we all wait silently.

"Any last requests?" someone from the back yells and it feels right, like we're all for the first time in decades hitting our cues. We feel light on our feet.

"A cigarette?" Birdie asks, and we all laugh, even Pete, a sound most of us have never heard before.

We oblige him, and I bend in close with my lighter.

He sucks in on the cigarette, and someone sets him up, *Tastes good.* "Like a cigarette should," he finishes. We want the moment to go on forever, we want it to be over in a second. Like children we don't know what we want. We are children, sheep, the emaciated skeletons being led from Belsen with our eyes melting from sunlight. That point at which even the natural world is a killer.

"A side proposition," he says. "To the one of you who held back just a little bit of his money, just enough for that last beer." The smoke rises over his eyes like a bridal veil. "The lighting is bad," he says, his head motionless. "Where are you standing?"

All of a sudden a twitchy little guy comes out of the crowd, closer to Birdie's feet. Birdie smiles, beatitude.

"All the money in your pocket for my last words," Birdie offers.

Hummingbird quick the man reaches into his pants and pulls out his money, pushing it into Birdie's shirt pocket. Birdie leans down and takes him by the shoulders, his lips so tender against the man's ears that they're like a kiss. I'm two feet away and for the life of me, the very life, I can't make out a god damned word. Like writing in sand. When he's finished he nods at the man, who retreats back into the human crowd.

It's over almost before we know it begins. I hand Birdie the gun, place a bar towel blindfold over his eyes and plant a kiss onto the sandpaper of his cheek. Then he raises the gun to his temple and squeezes the trigger.

Click.

It is the sound of a man's scrotum shriveling back into his stomach, evolution in reverse. The sound of a whole world thrown off its hinges.

Later, as we sit in a corner, just the two of us, Birdie having refunded at least some of the money as rounds of drinks, he plays with the gun again, his fingers wistful. Sensing it, I tell him he can try again, and he looks up at me with eyes so wet I know I've disappointed him. "No," he says again. "No. Not here, no."

It hurts to ask, but nothing I'll ever do will be so important again. "How many times before?"

"Eleven," he says, shaking his head. And then, when I am sure he isn't going to say anything else: "Do you have any idea of the logistics? To find the right bar at the right time. The ceremony. The girding of the loins. The helpmate?" He reaches over touches my elbow, tightly. "Eleven." And then, before I know it, he's gone. Like a magic trick, Santa Claus ascending the chimney. By nightfall the shift workers come in. None of us who were there ever speak a goddamned word of it. We cherish it. Hold it inside to warm us on the coldest nights.

He's right, you know. The logistics are immense. To find the bar, to know it instantly from its look or its smell. It's all about numbers, odds, percentages, but not the risks you'd necessarily think of. We were speculating, but we didn't quite get it right. In a better bar, sure there's the police, the decor as he said. But what it comes down to, ultimately, is the clientele. In a better bar people just couldn't abide the disappointment

SOMETIMES THE BONES ARE VERY BUSY

G.K. Wuori

Star Loon and the others listened as the mechanic man told them the truck would take hours and hours to fix, that he worked alone and might be interrupted frequently with business that didn't require him to goddamn delve into the ancient history of trucks or dig into every goddamn box, cubby, and cabinet he had in search of parts so old he'd have to wash the dirt off before he could goddamn grind the rust off.

So, he continued, this mechanic man, not an old man Star Loon could see, whose mouth smelled like carbon and fever, none of them could stay in the truck—Jesus!—since he didn't know if the truck would go up on his wobbly rack all by itself, let alone with seventeen people in back—granted, pretty light, pretty thin people—so they would have to get out. He would appreciate it, too, he said, if they didn't hang around and ask him every five minutes if the repairs had goddamn been completed yet. He thought he might be contemplating art with this repair and sometimes the only answers came out of your goddamn fingers, and he didn't think his fingers could handle any long conversations with people who seemed to speak more languages than he had channels on his dish TV.

When Star Loon asked their driver what they should do while the truck was being fixed, all he said was, "I don't give a shit. Just don't get yourself beat up."

"Why would we get beat up?" Star Loon asked.

Star Loon had, of course, no idea where she was, but she thought this violent land kept most of its violence in the cities, and there was no doubt they were far from any city, this village, she thought, where you could look down the road and see it from one end to the other, and where there was so much sky overhead that some of the women held hands constantly out of what they called a persnickety fear of falling right off the earth itself. Star Loon held no hands other than her own, but she understood how this weeks-long loss of all their usuals could make those women nervous, even silly at times.

"This is America," their driver said, "and a lot of people got views. You look funny, and it's damn straight you talk funny, and some of you got a smell, you know, which ain't your fault, but when the truck is fixed, we hit the road."

The man might have been more genteel, Star Loon thought, but he had a schedule to keep, and he kept telling them that, this schedule as much a burden to him as a terrible illness might be to someone else.

As the small group walked over toward an empty field and began to wonder if their distance was far enough so that mechanic man would not lose his cordial side forever—moving a few steps into the field, talking, then moving a few more steps before putting bags, and satchels onto the ground and sitting—the driver took Star Loon's arm and pulled her aside.

"That smelling business," he said, "about smelling funny—I didn't mean you, sweetheart. Well, I mean, I did a little, but yours ain't a bad smell, not at all." He laughed and then added, "maybe a little like oatmeal and coffee. Still, there's folks around who might see you as a good dream in the middle of their bad dreams so you don't want to take no chances."

Star Loon appreciated his concern about her safety even as she ignored it and gathered her skirts about her and picked up her cloth suitcase, a tattered thing of her mum's. This was a very cold place, this Midwestern place, and odd, too, since her wrinkled, oily map suggested that this Midwest was terribly far from the west to be considered in the middle of it.

On her feet Star Loon had only sandals, but she had to walk—a non-negotiable imperative—as though the priests were saying things to her, as though the moon had fallen on hard times. Star Loon had seven pins in each leg and she had been told they could rust, corrode, that she might find herself frozen like an electric tower, as elegant as a bare cherry tree, if she didn't seek out motion periodically. Pins, true enough, for a nine-year old, pins that were more like splinters in her adult bones, but bones, she knew had their needs and could not be ignored. All the others in this rickety-tickety group knew about Star Loon's bones. Even when they'd been on the one boat for the longest of all possible times, and there hadn't been enough room to think a big thought, let alone to walk for decent exercise, there had always been someone willing to push her onto her back and grab her legs and move them up and down and back and forth, always demure ignoring the necessary exposure of her personal muscles.

She'd been only nine when the men had crumpled her bones in their bare hands while her father screamed an incoherent repentance. He'd screamed apologies to the men—"curt bruisers" he'd called them—and then whispered apologies to Star Loon as he picked her up and saw how her legs flopped like cooked noodles. Later, he apologized to his wife and Star Loon's sisters. He apologized to his mother and an uncle as well as three teachers who'd always known he'd get into trouble someday. For a short time he'd gone around apologizing to all the dogs in the village, along with the chickens, the crows, and a small stream that had never been more than a trickle since Star Loon had been born. Apologies aplenty, Star Loon remembered, until there was no one left to receive his sorrow. Then he'd killed himself.

None of that—anymore—was at all worth thinking about.

Star Loon began the walk from the truck repair place into the town. Their driver, sitting upon a mound of automobile tires, gave her a dismissive wave with his hand as though he knew that in a very short time there would be so little left of her they could mail her home in an inexpensive package.

She walked swiftly and forced the motion until a rhythm came into her. Her breath puffed out of her mouth in frosty Midwestern clouds, the good breath of exertion and concentration, all the miles they'd traveled since days and days ago turning her muscles into sleeping sisters, her nerves into sticks. Sometimes her bones felt very busy.

The town seemed unhostile, if cold. Great houses of enshrubbed privacy were on both sides of the street, but there were shops, too, not far away, a long line of shops filled with promises and delights. Over here was clothing said to be pre-owned, and there a shop of bicycles where all the wording, the signs, were in another language, she thought maybe it was Spanish; a chemist—'pharmatique,' it was called—a petrol barn, a shop of three legal solicitors (not a good profession back home, solicitors marked for odd fates in the shifts of politics). She'd written a paper at the university one time about how lawyers should not be allowed to have families and she'd received great praise for her work. Now, however, all these years later, she could no longer remember what her point had been—probably arrogance, she thought, something about letting the world know that Star Loon had a marvelous future ahead of her.

Still, these shops, nothing terribly unfamiliar. She thought their driver had said the end of their journey was near, so she thought it was good to have an inkling of what her new home might look like.

A beer salon approached on Star Loon's side of the street. She thought a rich and tasty beer would be the soothing side of daring. If she brought sixteen bottles back to the truck with her she would be famous and greatly loved, someone who took the night and folded its edges over to reveal the sun. Of course, she had only enough money for one can of soup each day, that and the rental of the lizard man's can opener, so buying all that beer had to be only a wish toward a fine benevolence, perhaps a dream of madness. One good beer, though, would be as good as yet another can of soup so she walked into the beer salon. Very dark, she thought, maybe they were having electrical troubles, but there was a man behind the long table who looked at her.

87

There were other men, too, they looked like old men, and not many of them. They were sitting at tables and on tall chairs and they were looking at her along with the barman. She hoped it wasn't against the law for a woman to purchase beer. For a moment she felt like Clint Eastwood in an old-time movie world, though she supposed Clint Eastwood would not have worn sandals while riding his horse. When she was only a girl she had dreamed that Clint Eastwood had taken her off the mountain at home. He said she had to learn English if she would have his babies, but the English had been terribly hard and the babies hadn't come. Star Loon remembered how wretched it had been to disappoint such a fine man.

Walking up to the long table, she held out her hand to shake the barman's hand, held it the way Americans did, her right hand, fingers pointed, thumb up, although the barman only said, "Yes, honey?" and did not shake her hand.

"Do you serve beer?" Star Loon asked.

This made one of the men behind her laugh, and that caused another man to join his laughter. Star Loon thought for a moment that she'd just broken the law, and that now things might be very bad for her.

Bravely, she smiled, prepared to confess her error, but the barman only said "I honestly do. Yes, ma'am."

"Then I shall have some beer," she said.

She had an American ten dollar bill in her hand, and when the barman put the glass of beer in front of her he said, "That'll be ten dollars."

Very expensive. Star Loon wondered if she could live for ten days without any of the one dollar soups, if the exquisite warmth and good feeling of the beer would be exquisite enough. There was more laughter behind her, and Star Loon gave the man her money. Not at all naïve, she supposed they might be laughing at her. Perhaps they did not understand that there had been so little pleasure during these many weeks that she needed to feel it if only for a moment. Let pain predominate, she knew, let it go on and on and on, and eventually your mouth dried out and your kidneys shut down.

Perhaps, though, they simply thought her an alcoholic woman. Such women were always laughed at back home. The laughter made them cry and sometimes made them beat themselves with sticks. Star Loon wondered if American women might be like that.

The barman was smiling now and said, "For another ten, I'll put an egg in it."

An egg! They had talked of eggs one night when the sea had been calm. They had cooked them in their words and served them up in their sentences. They'd gone through turtles and snakes and doves and chickens until the steel container that was their shipboard home had growled symphonic ally from stomachs gone berserk not so much from hunger as from memory. They had all laughed, though, each of them saddened by distance, yet buoyed by the lizard man when he said, "I've heard their streets are paved with eggs."

Strangely, no one had attempted to rebut the lizard man, to suggest the technical difficulties of streets paved with eggs. It seemed enough, and fetchingly so, to imagine a place so wonderful the streets simply didn't have to be used. Grand murals might be painted on them, Star Loon imagined, painted on the highways from west to east, an arm of happy washerwomen keeping the pictures crisply clean. Good stuff these dreams, she thought, except we sometimes tell them to the children and turn them into restless traitors. I believe I am one of those children.

"Yes, please," she said to the barman.

The raw egg went into the beer like a golden fish diving through amber. An enchanting soup, Star Loon thought, food and the whizzing hymn of the tiny stars of alcohol. Now, though, it would be twenty days without food. Her poor stomach would clang like a bell tapping against her spine. She would be weak and pitiful, although some of the men liked a woman who was weak, as though she'd just had a child or been beaten for voicing bad views. She'd been told it was not legal to be beaten in the America, although she knew you'd have to be as naive as a baby to believe there was any government anywhere that didn't have its scofflaws. What industry could survive without the occasional laggard having his noggin bounced off a steel beam? What church? What marriage?

Twenty days. It could be more than that, because even though they would be at the industrial site, it was said it might be one or two weeks or more before they were paid money, and she had no more money, not a dime, not a peso or a euro to exchange for some food or, dream of dreams, tooth powder, perhaps the most microscopic bottle of scent. Star Loon had always been told she smelled very good, and she missed being told that. Thus, sometimes luxury had to make an entrance. There needed to be ribbons and tulle and brass instruments played so lightly they sounded like raindrops. She could ask for poets or dancers, too, certainly magicians, although you had to be careful to watch that line between dreams and greed. Anyway, a mere wisp of luxury: without that, the work, the hurting muscles, even the sand flies in the spirit had no purpose.

The salon was warm, the men cheerful and still laughing at her misunderstanding of their ways, and the tall glass of a moment's peace was in front of her. For these minutes, Star Loon thought, I will be saffron and diamonds. Then I will be poor, will be a beggar whose only power is that the men in the truck will bargain for me. As the Americans would say—an expression she'd already heard many times—I will be the deal.

I will be a good deal.

Star Loon sipped the beer and thought about all the men back home who were beer sippers, although some sipped the way a waterfall flows and their wives would have to burn furniture in the stoves and send the children out to find metal and plastic for the selling. Sometimes the children were injured—cut, poisoned, blown-up—when they did this, but even in ancient times children were injured—sometimes they were eaten. Everyone, too, whose ears weren't sealed with wax or happy tunes, knew that the old families sometimes froze their children and then cut them up to be used on the family fire. Thankfully, *that* was all history now, deep history.

As Star Loon drank and the beer warmed her she felt happy, so happy that she laughed for one moment, her smile like that of her father hearing good news from a financial man. This, her smile, seemed to bring tears to the barman's eyes. She hoped her laughter hadn't saddened him, though you never knew about the secret demons of sadness. They were everywhere and loved to leap onto a smile and twist it into the smirk of bad thoughts and terrible losses.

"Are you sad?" Star Loon said. The barman looked at her and shook his head.

He said, "You've traveled from a far place, ain't you?"

"Yes, I have," Star Loon said, "but it's almost over now. There is a factory, and I have been promised work. Some can't breathe in such a place, but it never bothers me what I breathe. My father always said I have the lungs of a whale."

"Oh," he said. "I know where you're going."

He looked over to the other men and said something Star Loon wasn't able to hear. There were groans, and several mumblings that sounded like, "Oh, Jesus." Before Star Loon knew what was happening, the barman was putting her money back down in front of her, and two of the old sitting men were standing next to her.

"It's almost time for me to go," she said. "We are riding in a big truck, and I believe the fanning belt and the water pump broke down. This truck should be fixed, though. Have I been here long?"

"If you stay here," the barman began, "we will take care of you. Right, boys? You can work and there will be money, and you'll live the good life."

Star Loon saw droplets of sweat on the man's forehead, and both love and worry in his eyes— affection, for her, but he didn't know where to go with it. There were things he wanted to say, but he had lived too long and no longer knew how to drop the oil onto a hot pan. She, herself, had been told to trust no one but keepers and contractors on their journey. There had been thugs. There had been miscreants, vain men who would tell you their cough was a song, their passing gas a lullaby. There had been advantages taken, too, and even, one life lost. Still, these men here, in this beer salon, had no anger in them that Star Loon could see. They looked gentle and wore clean clothes and she knew, had seen, that the town was very small. Evil could not hide well in such places, though Star Loon knew it could have disguises and deceptive faces.

"I don't understand," she said.

"Look, honey," the barman said. He put a big hand on top of one of hers. She could feel the heat from all his thoughts, and the tiny ice crystals of the few dreams yet remaining. "First they'll take your knees, then your hands. They will let you have babies, but your babies will be born covered with grease and ash."

Star Loon wondered about her knees and her hands, if there would be pain or ugliness. She'd known women whose hands had been so broken by work the women refused to come out of their houses. Some had starved.

The babies—well, her babies were at home. There would be no more babies, nothing emerging from her insides with the face of a workman.

"This is a hard place to work, this place?" she asked.

"Not here," a man behind her said, "where you're going. Frank is right. Stay here."

"What can I do?" she said.

"You are beautiful," the barman Frank said, "and we have no beauty anymore. It has left our hearts, it has left our bodies. Our wives were once beautiful, but we have traded that for comfort. Now there is a hole where beauty once was. A hard storm, like tonight, will find us talking about the beauty of the weather, but as you can imagine..."

Behind Star Loon a weak voice mumbled, "Yes, Yes," and Frank the barman continued.

"If you leave," he said, "not only will the beauty be gone, your beauty, but we will have sent you into ugliness and degradation. We will be monsters and we have never been that—tricksters, maybe, but never monsters. Our bellies will burn and our feet will ache. Honey, earlier we would have cheated you; instead, you have saved us. Ain't that the cat's meow?"

Star Loon took it all in, even the curious idiom at the end of the barman's speech.

She worried that her truck might be leaving, that the driver and the man named Buddy would be cursing her absence and saying what they always said when things didn't go as they should: "Well, what're you gonna do?"

She also knew they would search for her for maybe one minute. After that, she would only be numbers in a book in a column marked *Losses*.

Yet, these men, right here, they were so sad. It was all very hard to understand. She had her money back now so she could be neither bought nor sold and she would have soup until the American managers paid her. Everything was fine there. These men, however—she finally looked around and counted; there were thirteen—were not only admiring of her adorable features (awkward phrasing, she thought; I am unused to finding laudatory words for myself in this language), they also saw in her a certain finished part of the universe, a corner of smoothly-wrought perfection. Settled on her flesh like the words from old and crinkly texts were the scampering spirits of all things round and curved and delicious and memorable, an aura that never rested and that was shiny like the oil from happy fish. She knew it was not a bad thing to be able to make someone happy, let alone to make thirteen men happy. Star Loon, though, wondered why these men spoke so gray about their wives. Where had beauty gone such that comfort was seen as some kind of bad sister substitute? Weren't beauty and happiness and comfort all part of the same ...*world*? Wasn't beauty everywhere? Could they see it in her only because she was weary and from far away—vulnerable, piteous, wan—something they would tire of when the time came for her to grow fat or to lose her teeth?

"I will miss my destiny," she said as she slipped off her coat. "Sometimes you have to do that, I think, or the world becomes dusty and filled with small holes." She wore only an old and tattered slip beneath her coat, something light in case she had been thrown into the sea during the early weeks and forced to swim for a thousand miles. Someone behind her coughed and took her coat from her hands.

"There's always more than one," Frank the barman said. "Uh—this destiny business."

He watched her upend the beer, and watched the golden egg slide easefully into Star Loon, a slow and ancient hunger disappearing as the old men nodded in happiness and approval.

HICCUP TRICKS

Bruce Taylor

"It says in here," Jack interrupted Duke because everyone did and by now Jack had out the *New York Times Almanac* and *Desk Reference* which was, admittedly, only one volume, but we've all been in bars where you knew there wasn't even a dictionary. This place has a big one, as well as the Scrabble Dictionary, a stack of old *New Yorkers* and *People*, Jack's personal subscription to *GQ*, and the occasional *Star* or *Enquirer* and a copy of the *Oxford Guide to Opera* that probably somebody from the college across the river left here about a year or so ago.

"Right here it says," Jack's cheek cupped in the palm of the same hand he held his Parliament, the smoke spiraling blue into the wake of the big fan circling slowly overhead. "There was this guy in Connecticut hiccupped for sixteen years straight."

"I heard sixty." What Duke was told and what Duke heard everyone understood were often very different things.

"It says hiccups most often go away on their own."

"That's what they probably told that Poor Bastard who hiccupped for 50 years." No one could say 'Poor Bastard' like Duke could, he meant it as sort of a toast.

Doc hiccupped again, it was only recently they had stopped laughing every time he did.

"It says close your eyes and visualize a neon sign, like a movie marquee or that beer sign right there." Nobody had to actually look, or really close their eyes. "See the word THINK blinking on and off; concentrate on the sign and make the word blink as fast as possible. You'll stop."

"Stop what?" Duke seemed really to want to know.

"Hiccupping, you ass."

"What you do is scare them." Jack went on his own. Everyone, it seemed, was prepared to defer to the bartender given the subject at hand, but it was early yet. Sure most people do the sneak up behind you with the boo! thing. And poke you somewhere, maybe tickle you, if you get real lucky. Or they'll scream at you, and the people that do that are not just the ones you predict would, the ones that are sort of loud and in your face anyway. Fact is sometimes it's just the opposite, sometimes those really loud guys can get real quiet too, sometimes fast.

"It's usually—no disrespect intended—a little guy," Jack nods to Duke, and Duke nods back, "will get right eyeball to eyeball with you and just scream. Remember..." Nobody was completely sure who Jack was asking them to remember, so they all tried. "Later we heard David had been here since he got off work, and he got off early that afternoon because of the rain. So it was nearly eight by now and some of us had stopped in for that let's get a drink and figure out where we'll go for drinks drink, and maybe some dinner. David just won't stop, screaming at me, in my face, actually I'd stopped hiccupping after the third one, scream not hiccup, but that didn't stop him. Every few minutes or so he'd turn and scream, standing as tall as he could, one foot on the bar rail, and finally I have to scream back that "I DON'T HAVE THE HICCUPS ANYMORE." And then, guess what.

Duke said, "What?"

Doc said, "You got the..." and hiccupped again.

Jack said, "I got the hiccups again," and put his hand delicately over his heart and stood up straight in allegiance to it. "I swear to God."

After working sometimes six nights a week and drinking here all seven for as many years as he had, Jack knew everything there was to know about the bar and wasn't beyond making the rest up. One Sunday, before he got there that day, there was an impromptu contest for the best Jack story ever. It couldn't be just one he told but one that had happened to him, and it had to be verified by at least one other person.

You would have thought the winner would be the one about the owl dive-bombing his head, or his one time driving a car in the last twelve years. Or something from one of his yearly New York City art weekends where they take a bunch of college kids, and anyone else they can sell a ticket to, on a bus and stay real cheap to go to museums and shows which Jack of course only did a little of but the trip had become the maximum vacation he could regularly take on the skinny money he made, though nobody really knew, including the boss, how much he really made in tips, particularly on Saturday nights.

The Doc's favorite story about Jack was that he had three plastic inflatable fish, each about 18 inches long, two named for the obvious—"Blackie and Brownie" and the third, the grayish one he called Buster, sometimes Signore Buster. Once he had said if he ever had a pet it would have to be a fish so he wouldn't have to walk it, or brush it, but he'd probably end up killing it anyway and feeling bad, so that is how he got the fish, from three different people. And how it started one night when someone was going on vacation, Jack said he never got to go anywhere, so would somebody at least take one of his fish with them on their trip, and they did, and took a shot of Buster in front of the National Fishing Hall of Fame Museum with the two kids, standing right inside of the giant Muskies' mouth. Then everyone did. Sometimes you had to make reservations. So as a result Jack had by now a nearly full, meticulously annotated photo album of, Brownie in front of Sphinx, Blackie on the Great Wall of China, Blackie again, a favorite for some reason among the most upscale customers, at Stonehenge, lounging down the Nile on a tour, waterskiing. Too many cabins at the lake, winter hunting shacks, Tijuana, Cabo, Cayman Islands— lots of warm places that northern people have to favor, though Old John from either the Philosophy or Psychology Department across the river, always took turns taking them canoeing in the Boundary Waters, but he always brought them back. Jack had one rule, only one fish per trip, it was like, he explained, how the president and vice president never fly on the same plane. And all the saloons in between, however many blotto red faced people sitting around whatever table full of empties and no matter how they were held or placed, whether it was Brownie or Blackie—not so much Buster—all three looking like, somebody had to say it, like a fish out of water.

After a while some people thought it got to be like a family album—all those Christmases where nothing changes but the height of the children in front of the tree, the Thanksgivings' bounty endless and repeatable like a slow game of musical chairs, but every so often a person not the chair disappears. Except when he was alone, Jack mostly hauled out the album now when he knew a new guy enough to try to impress him. The boss might always be the mind and the heart of this place, but Jack was the soul. Doc couldn't even imagine if ever anything happened to him how many people would pass by for how long without thinking, there's the place Jack isn't anymore. But the story that won that contest was about the unfortunately overweight gal from the market across the street, who came in daily for a cigarette and a diet soda. "I haven't given her a diet soda in years," Jack had confessed to at least two other people.

"I try to keep my throat open," Duke moved his head back slowly, stroked his throat as if he were giving himself a large pill to swallow. "I try to sense when a hiccup is coming, then a second before it happens, I burp. Well, really it's a fake burp. You know when you swallow air." Everyone did and was absolutely certain, given the pause and the face Duke was making during it, that he was going to illustrate, everyone had seen him do it before, but he didn't this time. "It's not easy as you'd think. And dangerous too, you don't want to try it when you're eating."

"A burp hiccup, no, a burp-cup" John almost never said anything that wasn't out the side of his mouth, while the rest of him would make eye contact off the big mirror that lined the whole back bar, a mirror John always said was there so nobody has to drink alone. Nobody really thought he was even listening at all, as many stools away as he was.

You could pretty much find any kind of guy you need down here. Skip was the dentist, you went to Chris for insurance and Joel for glasses, Mike for building. If you had to have any fine work at all, used to be Hippie and Schelp for anything else, and everybody it seemed, would paint or lay concrete if they had to. John was the electrician which meant he could work pretty much whenever he wanted to, though lately he didn't want to much.

Hippie used to swear what works best is to tell the person with the hiccups. "Think of all the bald men you can." Though he had also heard someone ask, "What color is a white horse?" Hippie said you'd be surprised how many people paused a beat on that one, or even that Grant's Tomb thing though Hip was pretty sure that was just a riddle and not a cure for anything.

Duke seemed unfazed. "What I like is it's not uncomfortable, it's like the hiccup has its natural follow-through." He flicked a limply pointed finger towards both John and the Doc, the universal sign— at least down here—which meant he was buying their next. John nodded his thanks, Doc hiccupped again.

Suddenly there's three things for Doc to try to do together, not-hiccup, hold his breath as long as he can and, and three, now that a figure stepped through the glare into the dark bar, sweeping her sunglasses off with her left hand, jangling her keys with her right, tossing into the long shadows a small—what use to be honey—mane, he has to check out Nance's ass.

If anyone of them needed to say Nance had been the princess here some years ago, the other two would know exactly what he meant. There's always at least one even in the bad years, though a bumper crop was almost never more than three. They're always young of course, their version of a regular. They sort of adopt the place and the place them, which doesn't mean the old guys don't want to sleep with them, just part of being a princess is to be smart enough to never get drunk enough so you'd let them. Everyone knew that, if they often misunderstood it.

Usually they're a little girl that can fill the whole room up on a winter afternoon, down here when it's quiet; trying to study at the front table where that late sun comes in at just the right angle it looks like a spotlight and the whole thing can look like a painting, the whole winter afternoon.

Guys used to have long arguments whether Nance's ass was like one or two teacups. The Boss started that. Anytime anybody even mentioned Nance, and she got mentioned down here a lot for that first year or so, anytime anybody would even say her name, he would pretend he was sipping, hold his little pinkie up in the air, and peek, you know how you can, over the edge of the tea cup and do the Groucho eyes and no one does the Groucho eyes like he can. Jack couldn't stop laughing long enough to show us what he meant, so in trying to do so, tried to get his cigarette out of his mouth but it stuck to his lip, and he ran his fingers down the whole length of it, so ended up burning his two fingers, right there you know where you do.

Nance claimed that what they did at the hospital—she was a med tech there now, and with two kids so was only here every once in a while—was to slide a well-greased length of thin, flexible rubber tubing through one nostril to the point where it just barely touches the back of the throat. This was known as "nasopharyngeal airway insertion," and is believed to work by stimulating the vagus nerve.

The what nerves? Duke thought he'd rather have the hiccups, forever.

"The Chinese gently rub their ear lobe until the hiccups are gone."

Where did she get this stuff? She does, however, still look better in a pair of jeans than your average human being.

"Or you can hold your tongue with your thumb and index finger and gently pull it forward. That's what the French do."

As if that would carry any weight down here.

"Drink vinegar. Eat a dill pickle. A spoonful of Mustard." Duke was on a roll now.

"Sugar," John said.

"Honey, peanut butter, lime juice. Give the Doc a shot of lime juice...and put some Tabasco in it."

"Sugar."

"Maybe a lemon wedge."

"And put some sugar on it." John was not to be deterred. He put out his cup for some more coffee; he's sober now nearly five years.

"I'll give you five dollars if you hiccup again, right now!" Duke moneyed up on the bar a bill and slid it to the side not so far he couldn't slide it back. "Shit, I screwed that up, it was supposed to be, I'll bet you five dollars if you don't hiccup again. No." He paused and rolled his eyes and swallowed, "I bet you but five..."

Once Doc saw three guys get them at the same time, they can be contagious, like yaw or jokes about women, but at this very moment he couldn't tell anyone he had. These three guys started puffing on their thumbs, were blowing themselves up like balloons. And since they were in for their after game beer or twelve they were all dressed in these neon yellow jerseys with their names and numbers in a spangley silver. "The Soft-Ballers" their shirts read, now there's a name you can't see written enough across three fat men, all they needed were a bunch of other guys with ropes trying to hold them down.

"Listen to this," Jack's back in the book again. "Chew gum. Take a hot bath. Jump out a plane, I guess. Immerse your face in ice water, breathe through a wet washcloth. Have someone deliver a swift punch to your abdomen. Ow. Smell the fumes from a lighted candle."

"That's just like the matches"

"Put ice bags on both sides of your throat. Breathe into a paper bag."

"I thought that was for going crazy."

"Say 'pineapple.' Why pineapple? Stand on your head. Make yourself vomit. Oh? Talk non-stop for ten seconds. Look at this, it says 'stimulate your clitoris.' Then it says, in parentheses, '(Women)...'"

"I'd do that."

"Well I wouldn't." Sometimes we nearly forget that Jack's gay. You may say that about other guys, but Jack's really the only one you really do.

"It always works for me." Nance finished her tap to leave but didn't.

"Ok, here it is." Jack turns towards the large old dentist chair bolted to the floor at the far end of the bar. Harry's chair. Harry thought a chair that had that much pain in it, deserved a place where people weren't feeling any at all. Right behind the chair, above up on bar was a small headstone, most people thought it was real, said "Harry was Right". Doc was one of the few who could get away with sitting in it, at least in the afternoons. "Sit in a chair where you can lean far back, such as a recliner." Doc did.

Shoved way down under between the big chair and the end of the bar were two empty dog bowls. Wacky the bar-dog had no doubt more beef jerky and the occasional pickled pigs feet bought for her than any other animal in history. "At least in captivity," Duke was rumored to have added the first time anyone said this. So as a result Wacky was tubby enough that people often dropped by in the afternoon just to take her for an extra walk beyond the not long but labored waddle she and the Boss took every weekday night. When Wacky died the whole street mourned. Even Denny, the Barber who bought Red's Barber Shop but left the old sign he claimed out of respects, that cheap bastard. Jack's brother Jeff had never let anyone else cut his hair even in the hospital. Even Denny said it was a damn shame. A couple of the other bars in the street changed 4-6 to Wacky Hours for the rest of the week. On that streaming digital sign the bank had just down the block it read "We Will Miss You" over and over for the whole afternoon. The Boss himself was, of course, inconsolable.

"Close your eyes; tilt your head back as far as possible; open your mouth wide inhale as much air as possible." Doc had already been doing that for long enough he thought for a second he might pass out but then thought the better of it. "Visualize a hook. Jesus, a hook. A hook in the lower part of your throat and a ring farther up that the hook could catch onto. Look there's really a diagram."

"It looks to me the least of this guy's problem is hiccups." Duke seemed to be getting bored with all this which meant other folks would have been for awhile.

"Ever hiccup when you were high?" John said more than asked. "I mean it. Have you ever hiccupped when you were stoned, or heard anybody else ever?"

"Look at this," Jack swiveled so even if we couldn't see what he was reading, we could see that he was reading this right out of the book, his finger following along. "Hikop—hicet—hickok—another thing all together—look you can also spell it hiccough." Duke was thinking he might should go home soon. "Look, look at this, 'hickey: a gadget, device, a tool used for bending pipe,' so there's really a doohickey called a doohickey. Look 'a pimple or a pustule.' Not the way I do it. Look, there really is a 'Hicksville'." For this Jack had to turn the book all the away around. So everyone could see this for themselves.

PALS

Karl Elder

Pay day. But deeper in debt than ever. The car in Dad's name, but the loan was in mine. Lien: 4-door '60 Buick Le Sabre with fifty thousand actual miles. Though it set me back over seven hundred, she looked like a thousand dollar bill. Not a scratch. I spent the whole second shift glancing in her direction. I had no idea that a hunk of metal could produce such a welcome sense of independence. It was my first opportunity for a night on the town following my voluntary incarceration as an Illinois state employee. I decided to celebrate my reprieve from Camp Grant by violating an Illinois statute. The bartender drew me a Budweiser.

A small placard scotch taped onto a huge mirror behind the bar: *IF YOU WERE BORN AFTER TODAY'S DATE IN 1946 WE CANNOT SERVE YOU.* I sipped at my beer, looking myself in the eye, wondering if the bartender actually thought I was old enough or whether he didn't really give a damn one way or the other as was so often the case in the half dozen small taps I frequented up around Dekalb. Mirror, mirror, who the hell doesn't look twenty-one a half hour before closing time on a slow weekday night at the Crossroads Bar & Grill? Even the bartender appeared to be a novice, despite his near stupor. I hoped he wasn't too drunk, that he would remember me and set me up, no questions asked except, "What'll ya have?"

You good lookin' son of a bitch, I addressed myself, still studying the mirror—Shiller was probably right—you could use a trim. It was touching my collar, a sore point with the boss. I didn't want to sound uncooperative, but I reminded him that I was a supervisor, not a ward. He replied with his customary sense of diplomacy: "Get a haircut."

A coin trickled into the jukebox behind me, and Englebert Humperdink's false and pretty sentiment soon permeated the room. I ordered another glass and slowly became mesmerized by an electric Hamm's beer sign revolving with a plastic scene of the land of sky blue waters. It was attractive and accurate enough to remind me of my previous summer's canoe trip in Wisconsin except it lacked one important detail—the empties on the beach.

The Righteous Brothers soon stood in for Englebert, and I decided it was time for me to get a glimpse of the patrons. I swung my head around and caught sight of a blonde—middle thirties— or so—wearing a fall that didn't quite match her hair and sitting across from a male companion in a booth. Other than a lush called Charlie that the bartender was arguing with about the Cubs' chances of taking the pennant, the couple and I were the extent of the Crossroads' customers.

I flipped a quarter on the bar, dug a hard boiled egg out of a jar before me, cracked it and slowly salted it. I was bored, but the salt whetted my thirst, so I figured on one more before bed in hope the arm in the jukebox was reaching for something decent. No soap—Elvis. I made up my mind to swallow hard and fast, to spare my ears the drudgery. I nearly choked as I caught the reflection of Willard Jenkins tripping in through the front door, squinting at the back of my head. It was about to be an embarrassing moment for both of us since I was certain he knew my age. It dawned on me that I had him by the balls, though. There was no way he'd mention it to the bartender or anyone else. He was supposed to be taking a day of sick leave. His absence had required one of the daytime supervisors to work a double shift.

"Well," he said in an unusually jovial tone, enhanced probably by his own realization of the truce that was about to ensue, "dropped in for a quick one after work, huh?"

"Yeah, how you been feeling?"

He was loaded. "Doc took the stitches out today," he snorted. The bartender brought him a bottle of Schlitz, though I hadn't heard him order it. He thrust his hand deep into a front pocket, pulled out a roll of bills, peeled the top one off, exclaiming, "Keep it, Frank, you may be workin' some overtime tonight."

Frank mumbled something like "Thanks for nothing."

Jenkins chuckled and wobbled a bit on rubber knees, leaning on the bar. He held his beer in both hands, picking at the label with his thumbnails until it was entirely gone. Then he turned and stared for a moment at the couple seated in the corner booth before he looked back at me, and, again, he chuckled. The Elvis tune was winding down, and Jenkins picked up the chorus.

"Willie!" the blonde waved.

Jenkins waved back. "Hey," he said turning to me and clutching my wrist, "come on, I'll meet you up with a couple of pals." His breath was like formaldehyde.

I hesitated. The house lights flickered. "I don't know; it's getting kinda late. Don't you suppose Frank here wants to shut her down for the night?"

"Awwww, don't pay no attention to Frank. He'll stick around here all night long as we tip him. He likes it. Jus' ask 'im. Playin' with them lights to let us know the boss ain't payin' no more."

He ordered me another before I had a chance to refuse. We carried our beer to the booth, and Jenkins slipped in next to the blonde, slopping suds in the process. "Dot and Jimmy Boy" was what he called them. Jimmy Boy appeared stewed and rather pensive—for good reason. Jenkins kept his left hand under the table, and Dot seemed to enjoy it. I wondered if he managed to get a handful since at close range Dot was obviously shy in the meat department. Nice face though if not for the white wing-tipped specs studded with glass jewels. Sitting next to Jimmy Boy, I hardly had a chance to give him a second look. The way he toyed with his swizzle stick signaled his displeasure with our company. I wanted out, but had never abandoned a half glass of beer in my life and wasn't about to commence with the habit.

After a couple of more rounds, Jimmy Boy excused himself out of the corner of his mouth and stumbled for the john. Jenkins yelled to Frank for four more of the same and zeroed in on Dot's ear with a private joke. Jimmy Boy was taking one hell of a long time. I finally slid and settled further into the booth, occupying his spot. I decided to stick around, thinking I didn't want to miss what was coming next. I even polished off Jimmy Boy's gin and Squirt.

"Spose he's sick?" Dot said. "Maybe I oughta check."

"Give the kid a break," Jenkins slurred. "Probably beatin' his meat."

Dot's face gave her away. She was excited by the idea. I mused over why it was necessary for barflies to perpetually go through the ritual. Why didn't she and Jenkins just slip out in the car and perform one of those wham-bams. It seemed the verbal foreplay would become boring after a couple of decades at it.

"Well," I interjected into a spell of giggling, my inhibitions having progressively dissipated, "better go shake the dew off my lily."

Dot reached over and squeezed my wrist. "Give a look for Jimmy—O.K.?"

"You bet," I said, sensing her eyes still on me as I slid out.

I angrily pushed at the door but could get it only partially open. Jimmy Boy was seated on the floor, leaning against the wall, his body acting as a barricade. I used the Women's and returned to the booth where another glass of Bud awaited me.

"Jimmy's out of it," I said and sat down hard on the naughahyde.

Dot acted as if she didn't hear me. I slouched back into the booth, wondering how long it would be before I was in Jimmy Boy's state.

Dot asked Jenkins to play the jukebox. He got change from Frank and negotiated fairly well to the middle of the room, squinting and punching selections—the same three as earlier, it turned out, and in the same order. It occurred to me that the whole scene must have been an ancient rerun; otherwise Jenkin's feeble dexterity would have botched-up Dot's request. In the meantime I noticed something at my ankle, pretending not to, knowing full well it was Dot's stocking foot. Something quickened at my crotch as it dawned on me what her stare was about when I scooted out for the john.

The bitch is in heat, I thought, swigging another sip of beer. As I peered at the carbonation in the bottom of my glass, I debated whether I should return her call with a nudge of my foot as if shifting to a more comfortable position. The thought high jacked a bit of blood from my head and shot it straight for my groin. I wiggled. She responded. Suddenly I was completely erect.

The increased pressure of Dot's foot on my ankle when Jenkins returned enlivened my breathing. I didn't want to look up for fear the pleasant sense of frustration in my pants would deflate when I confirmed for myself the truth of the matter—in all probability Dot was what the kids in Camp Grant called "a stone cock teaser." There was no way even Jimmy Boy was going to get in her pants. Otherwise, Jenkins wouldn't be trying so hard. So, I was surprised when Dot agreed to Jenkins' suggestion that the three of us pull up stakes for a joint a few miles away in Ottawa called Spike's. It would remain open as long as there was a body leaning against the bar, Jenkins said. The county liquor commissioner hung there, so the owner never sweats being busted for serving after hours. Given my lack of an I.D., the idea of moving to a place where I might encounter the commissioner didn't fare too well with me. I momentarily made my mind up to split, but my hormones wouldn't have it. By now Dot's foot had worked its way up my pant leg, her toes nuzzling the back of my calf.

Jenkins' motive for dragging me along hit me just outside the front door—there were only three cars remaining in the parking lot, mine and presumably Frank's and Jimmy Boy's, since they had been there when I pulled in and Charlie the lush had already left in his. Jenkins had lost his license following a series of drunk driving charges. He hitched and sometimes walked to bum off the booze. I resented the idea of playing chauffeur, especially when the only foreseeable reward was a swollen head in the morning. Still, Dot was very adept at dangling the carrot.

"He'll fall asleep," she whispered at me and pointed to Jenkins, who was having difficulty maintaining his balance with his back toward us, watering one of the Crossroads' evergreens.

"Don't peek," he slurred over his shoulder, nearly falling into the bush.

"Poor Jimmy Boy," Dot giggled, leaning against the car, rolling the back of her head on the top.

Jenkins belched and turned, having obvious difficulty with his zipper. "Fluck Jimmy Boy. Jus' what he needs—a nice nurse like Frank. Who knows?—maybe the two of them can get it on."

I took the back road. There was one clear instant crawling out onto the blacktop that all five senses short circuited. I felt myself rising out of the dentist's chair following a particularly grueling session. Somehow the Novocaine had invaded my brain. I locked my elbows and drove stiff-armed until the seizure ceased. But my penis remained at attention, and despite that Dot's flirtation had only recently turned serious, there was more than a slight suggestion from the contents of my scrotum that I was about to contract a severe case of lover's nuts. While I struggled to blot out the presence of her thigh and buttock placed snugly against mine, I had the drunken notion I should tell her she could gain my admiration and respect only if she fucked me before the night was over. I recalled my frustration at Jimmy Boy for blocking entrance to the john. There was something subconsciously eating me. A subliminal goal that had been thwarted. That's it— a *condom*; I couldn't get by the sonofabitch to swap a quarter for a rubber. Without a rubber, I mused, I wouldn't fuck this cunt with Jenkins' dick. The mere thought that she could possibly have one buried with the gum wrappers in her purse transformed the heat in my lap into a sputtering flame. Spontaneous generation, I tried to imagine—humor, *anything* to divert my mind from its present focus of attention. I even tried to get clinical about it. I speculated upon the condition in which a wet dream might occur if the dreamer was conscious. Was it possible to ejaculate without having moved a muscle? I felt something like muted false labor as the base of my groin involuntarily contracted. An oncoming car momentarily had my dim-witted attention, but before it could pass, her head was lolling on my shoulder and her tongue was in my ear.

"Got a handkerchief?" she whispered.

"No," I lied and swallowed hard. "What for?"

"That's for me to know."

I realized she was fumbling at my belt buckle. I cleared my throat. "There's a brand new chamois in the glove compartment, but be careful of the light; it might wake up Jenkins," I said, nearly out of breath.

It took her forever to get the plastic off. My anxiety over the possibility of Jenkins coming to life was apparent in my driving—I slowed to a point that the speedometer barely registered, yet I was afraid to come to a complete stop, afraid that any significant alteration in the present chain of events might somehow leave me high and dry. We drifted in a kind of limbo as Dot and I exchanged dumb smiles while she continued to fumble with the wrapper. Her clumsiness was almost welcome. Though I didn't want a mess in my underwear, I had the notion she knew exactly what she was doing—transforming the throbbing anticipation of ejaculation into glorious agony.

I never felt more numb in my life than during the prolonged moment of orgasm. I was no longer mindful of the presence of Jenkins or even Dot, and the car had arrived at a complete stop, straddling a freshly painted pair of yellow lines. There was huge relief, of course, and remorse for having thought her a cock teaser, and I told her so. She seemed neither angered nor resentful; instead, she asked me where she should put the chamois.

"Shove it under the seat," I said.

She did, and then reached for her purse, withdrew a pack of Benson & Hedges, and lit one for each of us.

"Sorry the situation wouldn't allow for mutual participation," I lied, imagining microscopic corkscrews of some disease burrowing into my skin.

"Never you mind, lover; it's the wrong time of the month."

"Oh," I said.

They were the last words we spoke to one another.

FIGHT NIGHT

Robert Flanagan

Walking up Monroe Street to the Milburn Hotel and Lefty's Bar, Dad jingled coins in his pockets. Tonight's bout was for the crown Joe Louis gave up by retiring, he told Patty. The smart money was on Walcott, because remember how Jersey Joe got robbed in his shot at Louis? But Ezzard Charles had style and could sock. The Cincinnati Cobra. Wouldn't that be something, an Ohio boy world champion?

At Lefty's, they put two telephone books on a stool so Patty could sit at the bar. Above and behind the bar was a console model television set on a high wooden shelf supported by two-by-fours. The TV screen was round like a porthole in a ship.

Lefty was a small bald man with a thick yellow mustache that curled up at the ends. His white shirtsleeves were rolled up tight around his hard biceps, and he had an anchor and rope tattoo on his left forearm.

"Red McCandless," Lefty shook Dad's hand. "How you been keeping?"

"So far so good," Dad said. He laid money on the bar, asking for a draught and an orange soda, and Lefty went to get them.

"One of the best little fighters ever to come out of Toledo," Dad whispered to Patty. "Take a look at those ears. There's a cauliflower crop for you."

Lefty brought back their drinks and leaned his elbows on the bar. His ears looked lumpy, like oatmeal.

"Who you favor, Red?"

"I don't know," Dad said. "Ezzard's pretty quick."

"Walcott had Louis on the deck."

"Jersey Joe's no spring chicken."

"Charles ain't been the same since he killed Sam Barudi."

Dad grunted. "A helluva thing, that. The poor guy. Poor guys, both of them."

Lefty looked at Patty. "How old are you now, champ?"

"Eight," Patty said.

"So who you picking?"

"The Cincinnati Cobra."

Lefty laughed. "Chip off the old block, hey?"

Sherm Atkins, one of Uncle Jem's drinking buddies, said that was pretty sharp boy there. He moved down the bar to sit beside Dad, "You mind, Red, if I treat the little slugger here?"

Dad shrugged and Sherm bought Patty a bag of potato sticks.

"What's money for," he told Dad, "except to spread around?" He himself was living upstairs at the Milburn, he said, as he did when he had the price of a room, but he knew plenty who were hard up and sleeping in boxes. Many a night he let some fellow flop on the floor of his room for free. "You can do somebody a good turn, why not?" He took a sip from the shot glass beside his beer and asked how the city job was going.

"Like a baby buggy," Dad said. "Gotta push it, but it goes."

Sherm happened to be looking for work himself. Maybe Red knew of something with the city?

Dad looked down at the bar and sucked at his teeth. "The city hires you, they'll want their pound of flesh, you can bet your boots on that."

Maybe Red could put in a word in the right place?

"I'm no big shot like Mickey Kehoe," Dad said.

Still, if Red could.

Dad shook his head. "Kehoe got me the job, and I take my hat off to him, he's a good ward healer. But the city! Now, with the Democrats out, the Republicans in, they keep piling on work like they're trying to see just how much you can take. Keeping the time sheets for street repair, and then parks added on, and now garbage crews too. I'm telling you, a lesser man would have broken down by now."

Sherm said he'd take anything.

Then he was a good candidate for a city job, Dad told him.

Sherm bought a whiskey from Lefty but didn't ask Patty if he wanted anything.

A big man came into the bar, and Lefty poured him a coffee on the house. Everyone there seemed to know the man. How's it goin, Sni? How you keepin, Sni? Lookin' good, Sni.

Dad leaned close to Patty. "Sniffles," he said. "Sni for short."

People made way for the man, and he took the stool beside Patty. He wiped at his flattened nose with a dirty handkerchief. His left eye watered and its lid kept winking, and where his eyebrows should have been were flat shiny scars, like worms. His face looked like it had been hit with a baseball bat. He wiped his nose again, sniffling, and wrapped the handkerchief around his knuckles like a bandage. Patty tried not to stare at him but couldn't keep

121

from sneaking peeks.   How could someone get hurt so bad and not be dead?

"What do you hear from your brother?" Sherm asked.

Dad licked foam from his upper lip.

"What I hear," Sherm said, "they might spring him."

"Spring him? You think he's in prison? He went there of his own free will, and if he's got the brains God gave a gnat he'll stay there."

"He don't like it, what I hear."

"What's not to like?"

"The routine, the chow, the cottage sergeants..."

"Just what he needs."

"No man likes being bossed around."

Dad pulled back his head, looking at Sherm as if he'd only just noticed him. "And you want a job with the city?"

"Jem's a man likes to stand on his own two feet."

"Hell, half the time he can't stand at all."

"That's your own brother you're talking about."

"I know damn well who he is!" Dad tugged at his nose with a thumb and forefinger, the way he did when he got mad. "My brother, right, and I love him like a brother. But lemme tell you something, Atkins, straight from the shoulder. James M. McCandless has been a sponger and a free-loader all his born days. The bartenders there in the old neighborhood, Saint Pat's, they'd come to my father, Oh Captain McCandless, you think you could put a little something on your tab? His tab? Holy smoke! Here Jem was rushing the growler with a tin bucket— Captain McCandless wants beer for the home—and then drinking it himself out back. When he was still in short pants, this was. And my father, a Captain of Police, a man with a position in the community and a reputation to uphold in the community, he had to stand there and listen to complaints about overdue bills from saloon keepers who weren't fit to polish his shoes. But he'd pay up, sure, then take the strop again to Jem. But you can't change a leopard's spots."

Sherm said, "Well, I only thought you'd like to know."

"He leaves Sandusky, where's he think he's going? The Soldiers and Sailors Home is the best thing ever happened to him."

"Myself, I wouldn't know."

"That's right," Dad said, and turned to face the television.

When the main event was about to start, Dad dug out the two tens he'd taken from the rent money in Mom's red fruitcake tin. He slapped them onto the bar. Give him the going odds and he'd take Charles, he called out. Ezzard was his man tonight. Three men put down money. You're on, Red!

Sherm reached to hold the stakes, but Dad slid the pile across the bar. "Lefty, hang onto this, will you? Everybody knows you're on the level." He turned to Patty. "Now if we lose, which we won't, but if, let's not worry your mother about it. And if you want another orange or anything, just say the word."

The fight was being held in Chicago, the announcer said, Comiskey Park, home of the White Sox, twenty-five thousand fans in attendance.

This was something for Patrick to remember, Dad said; this was history. Tonight's winner followed Joe Louis as world champion, Louis who'd won the title from Braddock the Cinderella man who'd taken it from Max Baer who'd won it from Primo Carnera who'd won it from Sharkey who'd taken it from that kraut Schmeling who'd got his hands on it only when the fighting marine Gene Tunney retired. Dempsey, Willard, Jack Johnson, Tommy Burns, Lord, you could take it all the way back to Gentleman Jim Corbett and Ruby Robert Fitzsimmons and the great

John L. himself, champions all, and tonight's winner tonight would wear their crown.

When Walcott was introduced, Lefty said, "Arnold Cream!"

Dad told Patty that was Walcott's real name. "But when he started boxing, he didn't want his mother to know, so he took the name of the great old welterweight Walcott, from the islands."

It seemed funny to Patty, a boxer having to hide it from his mom.

"And Barney Ross," Lefty said to Dad. "Remember? Real name Rosofsky. Tommy Burns? Noah Brusso. And lookit Ray Robinson."

"Walker Smith," said someone at the bar.

Lefty made a gun of his hand, pointing it the man's way.

Dad said, "Charles favors Sugar Ray a bit, doesn't he?"

"You mean his looks?" Lefty said. "A bit, maybe. In the face I see some resemblance. But, Robinson!" Lefty shook his head, "Only man I ever saw who could strut while sitting down."

Ezzard Charles wore black trunks with a white stripe and white waist band, and Jersey Joe Walcott wore white trunks with a black stripe and black waist band. They wore high black shoes tied with white laces and with white socks showing above the shoe tops. The fighters were black, the referee white. Walcott looked bigger than Charles. Charles was darker and had a small mustache. Walcott was half bald and looked old.

At home with the radio, hearing Don Dunphy announce the boxing, Patty pictured fighters as wild men with steam coming out of their noses, like bucking broncos. But on the television Charles and Walcott seemed like regular people almost. They had muscles, and you could see that they were bigger than the referee and the men in the corners, but they didn't look as big as The Captain did in Dad's photo album. In a picture taken at Bay View Park while Dad was still overseas in the hospital after the battles of Belleau Wood and Chateau Thierry, Dad's Dad in his police uniform was helping to carry Jess Willard out of the ring after the terrible beating he'd taken from the draft dodger Dempsey. Willard was the biggest man in the picture, but The Captain was the next biggest.

The crowd was noisy, but the two boxers were quiet. They stood looking at their feet as the referee told them the rules. It seemed everybody at the fight was excited except the fighters.

When the bell rang Walcott came out of his corner, rocking his shoulders from side to side like a man walking a heavy chest of drawers into place. He flicked out a jab, and another, bobbed and rocked, then turned sideways to Charles and moved away in a sort of stroll, looking back over his shoulder to see if the other man was coming along. When Charles followed, Walcott spun around and threw a right.

"Jesus Christ," Sherm said, "if that shine's not a cutie."

The man was a master of the sweet science, Lefty said. He told Patty to watch Walcott's left shoulder. When Pappy dipped it that meant he was going to throw his Sunday punch, the hook. And brother, was it a beauty!

Between rounds the corner men washed off the fighters' mouthpieces and greased their faces and rubbed their shoulders and legs and Lefty set up drinks and made change.

Patty chewed at his fingernails watching the fight, then looked away. Dad was staring at the television, his face hot. He'd whistle or grin, then groan or shake his head. Once the men all let out a shout, and Patty looked up to see the boxers together

in a corner, arms swinging fast. He turned around
on the bar stool. Across the room was a painting of
a fighter getting knocked through the ropes and out
of the ring onto the people sitting at ringside. The
other fighter stood with his legs spread wide and
his left arm across his body like he'd just thrown a
big punch. Patty spun on the stool. Dad laid a hand
on his shoulder, saying Hey, hey, and Patty sat still.
Hearing a fight on radio was like listening to a story,
something you imagined, but watching one was
scary. You might see somebody get hit and go down
and not get back up by ten, or ever.

When the men were quiet again Patty looked at
the screen. The fighters moved about the ring,
staying out of each other's way. Ezzard Charles
looked sad almost, and Jersey Joe Walcott like he
might go to sleep. How could they act like nothing
was happening? The punches had to hurt. And
everyone was watching to see if they were scared.

"Fifteen rounds? Jesus," Sherm said. "They could
go thirty like this. Hell, I could!"

"You couldn' go one," Sni said.

"Bullshit! What's this, they're dancing is all."

Lefty said, "The Walcott Waltz," and some men
laughed.

"Well, if Joe's waltzing," Dad said, "then Charles
must be doing the Charleston." He rapped the rim
of a quarter on the bar, rat-a-tat-tat. "For my money
Ezzard's way ahead on points." He winked at a man
who'd bet against him. "For your money too, right?"

Patty looked at the bar mirror instead of the
fight, watching the men watching the television.
They lifted bottles and glasses, cigarettes and cigars
to their mouths. Smoke floated up in the light like
incense at Sunday Benediction. Patty saw his own
face, soft and pink, in a line with Dad's red one and
Sherm's yellow one and Sni's lumpy leathery one.

All down the bar the men looked really serious, like the apostles in the picture of the Last Supper.

He looked back at the fighters. He knew they wouldn't cry like kids when they got hit, but he was surprised they didn't flinch or back away. They just stayed where they were and hit back.

When Patty wore his Lone Ranger mask he made believe it kept him safe and made him brave. He thought that was how it looked with the fighters. They didn't wear masks on their faces, but their faces seemed like masks. Like a fighter using another name to keep himself a secret, except this was another face. Whatever happened, the fighter kept it stiff and still. Whatever he was feeling, no one else could tell.

The fighters stopped fighting, and the men at the bar booed or cheered. In the center of the ring the announcer reached up and pulled down a microphone on a long cord. He read the scores, 78-72, 78-72, 77-73, and said Ezzard Charles was the winner and the new heavyweight champion of the world.

A tall old man wearing rimless glasses, a vest and tie and tweed suit coat got up to leave. He wore the coat draped over his shoulders like a cape and stopped beside Patty's stool. With the Brown Bomber in retirement, he whispered, the manly art of self-defense was in sad decline.

Dad collected on his bets. "Let that be a lesson to you, gentlemen, don't bet against an Ohio boy." He gave Patty a dollar bill. "A couple of winners here."

Sni said you hadda hand it to Charles, he had slick moves.

Sherm said Louis coulda whipped both of them at once.

Sni said what the hell do you know about it?

Sherm said who asked for your two cents?

Sni said you lousy, mouthy lush!

Sherm said you punchy bastard!

When Sni dropped off his stool, Dad got up and pulled Patty out of the way. Sni put up his fists. Sherm, on the stool, reached out and gave him a shove. The big man stumbled back, wind-milling, and fell over a chair, making a loud crash.

"That'll be enough of that," Lefty announced.

It was enough for him, Sherm said, and no hard feelings. But they ought to put that squirrelly bastard in a home, out on State Street where he belonged.

Lefty came out from behind the bar with a sawed-off pool cue. "Atkins, you're a troublemaker. Take yourself on out of here."

"I'll go when I'm damn good and ready."

"You're going now," Lefty said, and rapped the butt of the cue on Sherm's left knee. It made a loud knock, but Sherm acted like he didn't even notice it. He drained his glass, stood and straightened the lapels of his dirty sport jacket. "I'm ready now," he said, and stepped through the doorway leading into the hotel.

Dad helped Lefty wrestle Sni up out of a tangle of chairs.

"You'd best learn to watch what you say," Lefty said. "And keep at your daughter's there. She takes good care of you."

Sni took a seat and Lefty brought him another cup of coffee.

"When I was right," Sni said, "I'da killed'm."

"Don't I remember," Dad said to Lefty. "He ducked nobody."

"Right," Lefty said. "He had a brave manager."

When they went outside, Dad wobbled a little. Woo, fresh air! They crossed Monroe Street, heading for home. Suddenly Dad turned around, took Patty's hand, and crossed back over.

Sherm stood leaning against a brick wall smoking a cigarette.

"What're you hanging around here for?" Dad asked.

"I don't answer to you."

"Leave the poor guy alone, he's had enough."

"Who said I'm waiting for him? Maybe I'm waiting for a city job."

"Oh yeah?" Dad edged Patty back a few steps. "Well, it'll be a cold day in hell before I put in a word for a rummy like you."

"Mister big shot. Big shit!"

Dad poked at Sherm's shoulder. "Go on, get outta here!"

Sherm kicked Dad in the shin.

Dad hopped back. "A dirty fighter! I should've known."

He made fists and shuffled around Sherm in a half-circle, throwing punches that almost landed. Sherm kicked out like a dog was trying to bite him, using the right leg while holding onto the left with a hand.

"Sure," Sherm said, "let your boy see you beat up a cripple."

"A bully is all you are!"

"A crippled war vet," Sherm said.

"Don't hand me that crap." Dad stood breathing hard, just out of Sherm's reach. "I heard what happened. You fell asleep on the train tracks."

"You're full of shit! I lost it to a Kraut sniper!"

Sherm yanked up his left pants leg to show a wooden leg. Not like a pirate's peg leg, Pat saw, but round and polished like a piece of furniture.

"You were soused," Dad said. "You never knew what hit you."

"That's the dirty lie your brother spreads around."

"Who says Jem told me? Everybody knows it."

"He's the one sleeps on the tracks. That wino! He gets his head cut off some night you won't see me crying for him."

"You leave my brother out of this," Dad told him. He glanced at Patty, then looked back to Sherm, jabbing a finger at him. "I catch you out sometime when I'm alone, you'll rue the day."

"Blow it out your ass, McCandless."

"You heard me, you stumble-bum." Dad took Patty's hand and they walked off. "That low life SOB. I'm sorry he was there tonight, Patrick. I'm sorry you had to run into his kind."

Dad was limping and Patty asked him if he was hurt.

"No no, it's nothing. My brother Jem may have his faults, but he's twice the man Sherm Atkins will ever be. Never let anyone tear down your family, Patty. In the end that's all you have."

They walked under the railroad viaduct where it was dark and Patty was afraid there might be something waiting for them there, but nothing happened.

Dad sniffed. "Sherm Atkins—kicking like a girl! To tell you God's honest truth, I'd forgotten all about that bum leg of his. He's lucky he's a cripple, that's all I've got to say. On the troop ship over to France, we boxed every night on the aft deck, marines against marines. A southpaw welter, I went 5 and 2. No easy matches either. Every man on that ship was a fighter at heart."

Beneath a streetlight he stopped to show Patty his moves, shadow-boxing and throwing flurries of punches, then stopped to catch his breath.

"It's pitiful really," Dad said, "that business with Sni. He's on queer street, you know, too many knocks in the head. You can push him off-balance with a finger, and once he gets going backward the poor guy can't stop."

He took Patty by the hand, and they headed for home.

When Patrick grew up, Dad said, he hoped he had better sense than to have anything to do with boxing, or for that matter bars and drinking.

THE GLANTON GANG

Lee Capps

Tanner stood on the sidewalk, with his hands in his pants pockets, trying to smoke a cigarette. The wind was cold and he had forty more minutes to kill.

Tanner did sales for a screen printing company, and this morning he'd been called into his boss's office. "Tanner," Boseman had said, unbuckling his belt, unbuttoning his pants. "I need somebody to kiss butt. I mean really smooch some ass." Boseman reached into his pants, adjusted himself, and began retucking his shirt tail. "You're my man, Tanner. Are you my man?"

Turned out the boys in the art department—for obscure reasons—thought "Eat More Pussy" made a funny slogan for the rough up of a pamphlet, and they forgot to change it before it was printed and shipped. Boseman needed somebody to drive to Richmond and keep the client from quitting them. Tanner was his man.

So here he was, and thus far the only ass he'd smooched belonged to a Kelly girl. He'd had to lick boot just for a chance to grovel. It was enough to burn him up. But Christ it was cold.

He looked back at the office building. The glass door was lighter and scarred where it had been scrubbed, and you could still read the graffiti just fine—if you could read graffiti, which Tanner couldn't. The words were more Lucky Charms than alphabet soup—all diamonds and stars and lucky fucking clovers. Damn illiterate teenage gangs, loose upon the town.

He decided he couldn't sit in that waiting room. The magazines were all *Architecture This* and *Something Something Art.* And he didn't want to wait in the car after sitting on his hemorrhoids all morning. He flicked his cigarette into the street and watched a woman in an evening gown and a fur coat and an actual, honest-to-god feather boa come around the opposite corner and disappear down some stairs.

What the hell. He had more than half an hour to kill. Tanner waited for a produce truck to pass and loped across the street.

The sign was in French or Italian or something, but what it was was a restaurant. The woman in the feather boa hung her coat next to a booth and sat down with two or three other expensive-looking ladies. Tanner stood just inside the door, unbuttoned his coat, and combed his wind-mussed hair across his scalp. He slid the comb into his back pocket and walked over to the bar.

The bartender, a little wisp of a boy, was washing glasses. He nodded once at Tanner and looked down at his work. In the mirror, Tanner saw the woman with the feather boa and her three friends. They were more girls than ladies, he saw. Mid to late twenties. At least one of them had a big, sparkly ring. One of the girls met his eyes in the mirror and said something to the one next to her. She laughed. They all laughed, loudly.

In the back of the restaurant, among the tables, a thin blond woman with a concave chest whisked the carpet. She advanced by short, furious thrusts, like a sword fighter. In the corner a short, frizzy-haired man plinked out anonymous piano music. He looked over his shoulder and gave Tanner the uninterested stare of a cow, then turned back to his piano.

The bartender dried his hands on a towel and looked at Tanner. The boy had deep creases down from the corners of his mouth like a marionette. He looked whipped and beaten about by the world.

"Bourbon," Tanner said. "And a light beer." He peeled a twenty from his cash clip and laid it on the bar. When the boy set the drinks in front of him, Tanner said, "Trying to warm up" and downed the shot.

"Yes, sir." The boy made the change and replaced Tanner's shot glass with the money.

"Colder'n a Jew on judgment day," Tanner said, smiling.

"It's a cold day, sir." The bartender went back to the sink.

Christ. Tanner sipped his beer. Shouldn't have said that about the Jew. He didn't mean anything by it. It was just an expression. He looked at his watch: thirty minutes to kill. Tanner drank his beer and listened to the girl-talk. He could only make out a word here and there. He thought he heard someone say comb-over. His face got hot, and he pressed his palms against the top of the bar to keep from touching his head. He'd always combed his hair this way. Was that a comb-over?

The girls had gotten quiet, and he snuck a glance in the mirror. They were leaning forward in their seats, staring at his face. When they saw him peek they burst out laughing.

Tanner shifted on the bar stool, and his coat went tight across his shoulders. The bartender was reading, some kind of school book, looked like. "Hey," Tanner said. "You aren't a Jew, are you?"

"Sir?"

"You know. A Jewish-type person. Because I don't have a problem with it if you are."

The bartender had this blank look.

"It's just," Tanner said. "I feel like we kind of got off on the wrong foot, and all I'm saying is it was just an expression, what I said about Jews."

"Yes, sir."

"I'm sure you'll—if you are Jewish, and I'm not saying you are—I'm sure you'll be as warm as the next guy."

"Thank you, sir."

"On Judgment Day."

"Yes, sir."

"So are we square?"

"Square, sir."

"Great," Tanner said. "Good. So how about another beer."

"Yes, sir."

He'd never been called sir so many times in one day. It was like talking to a goddamn robot. Colder than *a robot* on Judgment Day, Tanner thought. How's that? While the boy was pulling Tanner's beer, the woman with the feather boa came up to the bar. She had eyelashes like spider's legs, slow and stealthy. "You're not from around here," she said to the mirror.

"How can you tell?" said Tanner.

But the bartender came up with the beer, and she said to him, "Eddie? Our little waitress has disappeared. Where is our little waitress?" Someone in the booth chortled. Or snorted. The woman in the feather boa seemed nearly in tears.

"Your server's in the kitchen," said Eddie the bartender. "She'll be back."

"Eddie," she said. "I won't lie to you. These women need drinks."

"What drinks do you need, Miss Glanton?"

"I don't know." She looked back at the table. Someone snorted. Or chortled. She looked around Eddie at the bottles and shelves. "What's on that bottom shelf down there, Eddie?"

"The drinks are on the top shelves."

"Eddie, what's down there?"

"I don't know, Miss Glanton."

"Well, why don't you take a look, Eddie?"

Eddie nodded once and bent over to look at the bottom shelf. Glanton leaned across the bar and flicked one end of the boa like a frustrated cat flicks its tail. Tanner couldn't believe it: she was checking out the bartender's ass!

Eddie stood straight and said, "There's a box on the bottom shelf."

"Eddie," Miss Glanton said. "I'm losing patience."

So Eddie bent over once more. She slapped him square on the ass, and he straightened up, holding a rattling box. Someone pounded the table and the glasses banged and the girls went on like a TV laugh-track.

Eddie pressed his butt against a cabinet. "Glass ashtrays." He held up a small, glass ashtray. "We used to use these ashtrays."

"I'll take that," Miss Glanton said and snatched the small, glass ashtray. "We'll need a margarita pitcher, Eddie. And glasses. With salt this time, Eddie."

Tanner watched her flounce over to the booth and sit. A red-headed girl winked at him, and Tanner stared at her, hard. He stared at her and took a long drink from his beer. She held his gaze and showed her teeth. Tanner turned slowly back to the bar. Eddie had put the ashtrays away and was shoveling ice into a blender. Tanner said, "What kind of place are you running here, buddy?"

"Sir?"

"Don't *sir* me. She slapped you on the ass, man!"

"Yes, sir." He made the margaritas and set the pitcher and glasses on a tray on the bar. The waitress was back. She took the tray into the hollow of her chest and inched it over to the booth like a caterpillar.

The bartender was reading his school book again. "Listen," Tanner said. "Buddy. Somebody ought to run those girls out of here with a baseball bat."

"Yes, sir." He turned the page.

"'Yes, sir.' Is that all you can say? Do something."

Eddie turned a page of his book and for the first time looked Tanner in the eye. "These ladies," he said. "Are *very* well-connected."

"Shit," Tanner said and shook his head.

Eddie's eyes were back to his book. "Yes sir," he said. That's all he would say. Yes, sir. No, sir.

So Tanner just drank his beer and killed his time through more giggling and foolishness. One girl pushed the piano player away and began bashing out either "Great Balls of Fire" or "School Days" and the red head sat on top of the piano with her skirt hiked up to her hips and her legs spread wide singing opera in German or Italian or something. Tanner acted like nothing could bother him. He had his own humiliations to deal with here in a few minutes. He couldn't be stopping to help these people.

Then he felt his comb slide like a snake up out of his back pocket, and he looked at the mirror in time to catch Miss Glanton drag his comb backwards through his hair. He ducked his head, but his hair stood above his bare scalp like a wave above the trough. The girls laughed at him, and the bartender read his book. Miss Glanton put Tanner's comb on the bar and looked him in the eye.

Tanner wiped his hair back across his bald spot with his palm, but before he could say anything there was a crash. The girl with the concave chest stood by the booth, streaming water like a gutter spout. One of the girls had dumped the pitcher on her. Miss Glanton dived at the waitress's feet, scooped up ice and began winging it at another girl, who jumped behind the bar to pitch ice from the bin. And Tanner couldn't believe it. The cheese dick bartender was still pretending to read. Tanner drained his beer and called to the bartender. "Hey! Hey buddy!" he said, in a voice loud enough to make it over the piano and yodeling and girl screams and laughter. "I want to buy another drink for that young lady." He pointed at Miss Glanton, who was now stuffing ice down the sobbing waitress's shirt. "That is," he said. "If she *is* a lady."

Miss Glanton looked up at him and dropped the waitress. The place was quiet now except for the sobs of the waitress and the gentle patter of the ice she scooped from her superfluous brassiere. Even the bartender was watching now. Tanner nodded at him, and the boy automatically made a bourbon and ginger and set it on the bar nap. Glanton tossed an end of the boa across one shoulder, bellied up, and took the drink. "Oh, I'm a lady, all right," she said and gulped at the bourbon.

"Well, since you're a lady, I'm going to share a little advice," Tanner said. "I don't know what these people are willing to put up with." He nodded with disgust at the waitress still on the floor. "But you don't know me. You don't know who I am or where I'm from." He said, "I just got out of prison for beating up a 'lady' like you. So my advice to you and your little friends is you be more careful who you're messing with." He stared hard at her again. It was so quiet you could hear the bartender's pulse racing. Untouched, the pages of his book flipped slowly closed.

Tanner hadn't been in jail since he was eighteen and got caught stealing road signs in Myrtle Beach. But for all this woman with her feather boa knew it was gospel truth, and for the moment, Tanner more or less believed it himself. For the moment, he could see himself in the passion of his pretended violences, the prison cot and shower play.

Then he reached out and plucked a feather from the boa. It lay in the palm of his hand, a desiccated insect. He said, "I have to go take care of some business, but when I get back I better not find you anywhere near this bar." He blew the feather into the woman's face, and he turned and walked to the door. It was fucking beautiful! It was quiet, like the whole room held its breath, and he'd have given anything to see the expressions on their faces.

Olivetti took the stranger's glass to the sink and watched him shamble out the door. He hated to see the sorry son of a bitch go. For such a bigoted, old loser, he had a certain used car lot dignity. And he drew some of the fire from poor Eddie Olivetti.

It couldn't last. The moment the door shut behind him, Miss Glanton started laughing hysterically and flicking the ends of her boa as if to stave off a fit. And Miss Barton said, in a deep voice, "I better not find you anywhere *near* this bar" and stuck out her chest and took wide steps for the door. And Miss Handy called from the piano. "Eddie," she said. "Eddie! What size shoe do you wear?" And Miss Glanton found this so funny she sat down in the middle of the floor, nearly out of breath and Mrs. Arrington-Dunn had the small, glass ashtray in her hand and her hand cocked behind her ear saying, "Tell us, Eddie! Tell us by God your shoe size or I swear I'll lay your head wide open."

Olivetti looked at the clock. He had two more hours to kill, and the small, glittering, glass ashtray was coming for him.

THE CASTLE

Molly Hoekstra

Tonight I get to work the best room in The Castle. It's not called The Castle, really, but that's what it looks like. Something out of a dark fairy tale, where the princess is held prisoner but gets saved and goes to live in a nice, bright castle with flowers and birds. Two stone lions guard the entrance, and there is a huge staircase that slopes around leading upstairs, to multileveled rooms and dance floors. A thin narrow staircase leads to the basement, which is cluttered with pool tables and video games. I think it used to be a library once. Now it's a bar.

Usually I end up working in the dance room, which is the worst. I have to push through people and big poles. I like to watch the people dance. They look ridiculous. But they really have no idea how funny they look, because they either take themselves too seriously or they are drunk. When I work, I don't drink like some people do here. It's far more interesting to be sober. It makes me feel better to look at the fools on the dance floor and be happy that I'm not going to feel embarrassed tomorrow morning. But tonight I don't have to watch anyone dance. The tables in this room are far apart. Tonight I can breathe.

Howard, the bartender is kind of a sadistic guy. He is middle-aged and single, short, bald and has a moustache that grows long and out like an old-time barber. He wears stupid suspenders with a matching bow tie. He enjoys being mean to girls he works with. He thinks he has to "break them in." I guess some people take their power where they can get it. He'll take his time making drinks when we have an order and yell at us if we call our drinks in the wrong order. Most of the girls kiss up to him. I don't. I don't care if he yells or takes his time; I'll be damned if I'm going to let him get his kicks watching me crawl for a Seven and Seven.

So far, the room is dead, and I'm scared this night will be a wash. I just want to get home to my cat, Aurora. She's such a good cat. She hears my footsteps when I come in, and she'll meow while I unlock the door. I live in a room that has a bed that pulls out of the closet. Usually I'm too tired to pull it out, so Aurora and I will just lie on the floor together watching Maury until we fall asleep. I was hoping to be able to take a cab home tonight. I only do that if I've done really well. Usually I take the bus. Sometimes it's kind of creepy, but then I start talking to myself out loud, like I am crazy. People tend to leave you alone if they think you are crazy.

Yesterday was my night off. I was walking down the street, and this guy pulled up in a car and asked me if I wanted to go for a ride. I said okay and got in the car. I was bored. I told him that if he touched me I would kill him. I said it in a crazy voice. I knew he'd leave me alone. We drove down to the beach.

He asked me a bunch of questions, and I made up a bunch lies. I think it's okay to lie to strangers who pick you up in cars. He was kind of chubby, worked as a pizza delivery man, and lived at home with his mother.

He didn't drink or smoke or do any drugs. He seemed like potential serial killer material to me, but that was OK because I want to be a psychologist someday, and I think it's a good idea to study these people. We talked for a while and looked at the waves. He was thinking about getting his GED. I told him I thought that would be a good idea. He said he'll never do it, though, because he had no faith in himself. I find it strange that people will always tell you exactly what is wrong with them. You usually don't even have to listen to catch it, but if you don't pay attention when they tell you, it's no one's fault but your own. A few minutes later I told him I wanted to go home. He drove me to an address that I made up and when he was gone, I walked around some more. Then I went home to Aurora. She was happy to see me. I guess getting in cars with strangers isn't the brightest thing to do, but someone is watching out for me. I can feel it. Besides, getting a little close to danger sometimes is better than being bored.

A bunch of businessmen come and sit in my section. They are wearing nice shoes. Christie says that's how you can tell if people spend money. Anyone can own a suit. Christie and I are the only waitresses with big chests. Everyone else is skinny and flat-chested. Christie and I also have the same last name, which I find really strange because it's not exactly common and we aren't related. I guess it wouldn't be that strange if we didn't have the same chest. But two coincidences mean something to me. We both get bothered about our chests all the time.

It doesn't really bother me if people say stuff, as long as they tip me okay. Christie says it only bothers her if they say it to her face. She doesn't understand why they can't wait three seconds until she is out of hearing range. I understand though. Some people are sadistic. They like saying rude things when they know you have to smile and kiss ass anyway in order to eat. Just ask Howard. But having a big chest means that I don't need to act cute and peppy. I don't need to flirt, although I probably couldn't if I tried. I don't have that type of blonde, bouncy energy in me. So I just talk in a low voice and meet someone's glance occasionally and that seems to work.

I also don't care if the drunk men touch me. Nothing overtly sexual or anything, just maybe putting their hand on my shoulder or not moving when I have to pass by so our bodies brush against each other for a second or two. I think lonely people sometimes need to touch someone just to make sure they are still there. I never touch anyone if I can help it. I don't like to invade people's space. Most people are oblivious of the space that surrounds them and keeps us separate from one another. Or else they just don't care. I don't know. If anyone gets out of hand, Troy will usually take care of them. He's a manager here, and all the women that come in here think he's gorgeous, which I find really hysterical. He has this accent that's either English or Australian, but I think he's an American. He has blonde hair like a plastic doll and blue eyes which the ladies love. They are so light, I think they are kind of creepy, like a spaceman. I told Christie that, and she thought I was right on the money. People here call me by endearing terms like Honey or Baby or Sweetie which is annoying, not because I'm a feminist or anything but because it bothers me how carelessly people throw around words that really should be for someone special. Troy calls everyone Love, which is worst of all, as far as I'm concerned, but women fall for it anyway. Maybe I'm just too literal, but I know Troy can't love us all. If any of the touching gets out of hand, Troy will say, "Don't touch the waitresses." That usually works, because I think people are embarrassed to be reprehended in what is supposed to be a higher-class club, but if it doesn't, he'll call one of the security guards. He says he likes to leave the "rough work to the big boys." So much for Troy's love. I don't think I will have to let these business-men touch me, though, because they will usually tip well anyway in a group because the company is usually picking up the tab. They have to show off to their co-workers, which is really funny because if they were here alone or with a date, they'd probably be cheap. Plus, taking a second look, they seem quite young. They also seem already quite drunk. The two youngest ones seem to be in charge. One of them is short and the other is tall and skinny. I will remember them all night as Short and Skinny. It's not that I like to stereotype people or anything; it's just because it's easier to remember whose drinks go to who. I walk over to them, and they order some champagne. "Celebrating something?" I ask in my low voice.

"We just closed a five-million-dollar deal," Short says.

"Wow, that's terrific," I say, like I am really impressed. And I guess I am a little, considering I'm hoping to clear fifty dollars tonight, but when you're dealing with big business, five million dollars doesn't seem like it would be a great deal of money. Maybe it is. Maybe I'm just young and stupid. Who knows? I go tell Howard about the champagne. He's really mad because the champagne is in the basement, and he will probably have to go down and get it

147

because the other bartender in the room is new and doesn't know where it is.

"Tell them to order something else," he says.

"No way," I say and walk away. Howard will probably take his time getting the champagne, but I don't care. I go and talk to the happy businessmen. They are so excited about their deal that I am kind of getting caught up in it. Tonight, I think it would be nice to celebrate with the young people. Actually, the young people are probably several years older than I am. I'm only twenty, but I can't tell anybody that because I would get fired for being underage. But most of the time, I feel old. Maybe it's because I run around all night, waiting on obnoxious people. I'm hoping I'll feel younger as I get older, but it probably doesn't work that way.

I meet the rest of the group. I run to the other bar to get drinks for them until the champagne comes. One of the group is feeling ill, so I bring him lots of water. I am everyone's friend, which is a joke because I have nothing in common with any of these people, except that it turns out Short went to the same high school I did, which I think is a strange coincidence. We didn't know each other or anything because he is six years older than me. Then he went to MIT and now works for this company.

After the champagne arrives and the sick have been tended, I am no longer needed. One of the men is sitting off to himself, at another table. He is an older man. His beige suit sets him apart from the others in their dark blues as much as the white in his hair. He asks me to sit down, and I do because I am tired, and Troy isn't anywhere in sight. I need a cigarette, and this man looks like the kind of person that wouldn't care if I lit up. We talk for awhile about Aurora. Some people think you are strange or boring if you talk about your cat a lot. He doesn't have a cat, but he used to have a dog, so I

think he understands. I ask him if he got any of the
champagne, and he lifts the glass a little.

"Scotch," he reminds me and I nod. "The
champagne is for the boys. They think this is a big
deal. They are young, you know. It's a lot of money
to them."

"Yeah," I say, like I know what he means. So I
was right after all. Five million is a drop in the
bucket.

"That one over there," he points to Skinny. "He's
never been out with a woman." His voice is a little
too loud.

"Really," I say, looking over at Short and Skinny.
They are talking to two girls who are wearing a lot
of makeup and dressy skirts. Short waves me over,
requests two more glasses for the ladies. I go behind
the bar and get the glasses myself, so I don't have
to ask Howard, who is sulking about not having any
customers. He yells at me for going behind "his bar"
and then places the glasses down so hard I worry
that they will shatter and the broken glass will fly
up in both our faces. They don't break, but when I
lift them up out of Howard's hands, he holds on to
them and won't let go, like an obnoxious sibling who
won't give up the candy he's supposed to share.
That's what I get for trying to be nice. "His bar" my
ass.

I bring back the glasses and pour champagne
for the girls. Short whispers in my ear, "They want
us to dance." His hand is on my arm. "Well, you
better do it," I say, "at least for the sake of your
friend," indicating Skinny, "considering he's never
been out with a woman before."

Short looks puzzled. "Did Tully tell you that?" I
nod. "Oh, don't even listen to him." Short laughs.
"He's not even for real. They just keep him on
because he's been with the company forever. He
sits in his office, and I have no idea what he does

all day, but it's certainly not anything important. Of course, Chuck's been out with a woman. He's practically engaged to his girlfriend." I don't ask Short why his friend is hitting on one of the girls when he is "practically engaged." I don't want to hear some dumb rationalization. It kind of makes me sick. I also don't like the way he talked about that old man. He calls him by his last name while Skinny is "Chuck" to him. The two couples go out to dance, and I kind of wish I could be working the dance bar right now, just for spite, just for Tully. It probably would be quite a show.

I go back to Tully. "Well, they are dancing," I announce, taking a seat.

"That's nice," Tully shuts his eyes. "Those boys," he sighs, "are good boys. They should be having fun." He looks away from me. "I had a son once," he says, then picks up his empty drink and chews on a piece of ice.

"Need another?" I ask. He nods.

The couples come back, ready for another drink. The boys are kind of sweaty.

Short suggests another bottle of champagne. "Are you sure you don't want to do some shots?" I ask, which I have learned is a direct challenge in this weird businessman drinking code. I actually just don't want to ask Howard to get more champagne. Even if he is a jerk, he's not making any money tonight, and I kind of feel bad. It's hard enough to come to work at some shit job every night, but to leave with nothing is the most inane type of failure.

Short and Skinny opt for tequila, and I suggest some White Zinfandel for the girls.

As I am leaving the table, some of Skinny's drink spills. He and I start to clean it up at the same time and our arms bump together. One of the girls says, "Let the waitress clean it, Chuck—it's her job." Which is true, it is my job. I clean the spill and head for the bar. Howard is grumpy about making the shots because he has to cut up a lime.

"It was going to be more champagne," I say. "But I suggested this instead."

"Don't do me any favors," Howard says bitterly. I give up.

I wonder what Aurora is doing now. I wonder if she is looking out the window. Sometimes Aurora and I sit and look out the window together. There is not much of a view outside my window, just the off-white rows of bricks and dark windows from the next building. I don't know what she sees that makes her want to sit there so long, but I try to see it. I wonder if the lady in the alley is screaming yet.

Behind the building where I live there is a sort of halfway house for emotionally disturbed people. A woman who lives there comes out at night and starts screaming. Sometimes I sit in the chair and open the window, trying to hear more of what she is saying. She screams about a man, or men in particular, I guess. "They are all fucking assholes," is one of the phrases I can decipher. I sit there smoking, feeling the night air coming through the window. "Idiots—all men, all of them," she says. Sometimes I have to agree. But I think human beings in general can be idiots. I used to think there was supposed to be this unspoken sisterhood between women, but I've learned by the way women customers treat me, cocktail waitresses are somehow excluded from the united front. In fact, one night when I first started working here, as I was coming home around Five in the morning, I passed by a businesswoman leaving her apartment who started calling me all kinds of terrible names. For some strange reason, I tried to explain that I have to dress the way I do for work.

151

"You are nothing but a slut," she said. I have to admit, I was shocked. I don't know why I was so personally offensive to her. I know better now. There is no sisterhood for people like me. I am on my own.

I bring the couples their drinks, and as I walk away, Short comes over to talk to me. "You've been really great tonight," he says. "We will be sure to tip you well."

"Thanks," I say, but feel more like thanking God I can truly relax now. I don't care if I'm a good waitress or not, although I know I am, which is kind of sad if you think about it, to be good at something useless. Short and I talk a little bit, and then he asks me if want to get together sometime. I tell him I don't go out with anyone that I meet here, which is my standard response and is pretty much accurate. I think that someone that I could truly like would never set foot in a place like this. He says that he is exempt from my policy because he would never be here if it wasn't where the whole office crowd wanted to go. I think that someone that I could truly like would never go out with the office crowd. I look over at Tully who is looking down at his drink. Short notices and laughs about how Tully always gets plastered at these company things. I think that someone that I could truly like would not make jokes at an old man's expense. I avoid giving him an answer. Then, we get to talking more and it turns out his apartment building is just a half a block away from mine, which I think is a truly strange coincidence because we live in a big city. First high school, now this. So I say yes, he can call me, because two coincidences mean something. Well, actually, that is only part of the reason. Another part is that it will get me out of my miserable apartment for one night. And another part of the reason is that I know I must be a lonely and desperate person myself, to agree to go out with Short, because there is nothing about him that I really like. Lonely and desperate people make lonely and desperate decisions that have little to do with what kind of people they really want to be. We go back to the table where Skinny tells Short that the girls want to go out to another club. Short looks over at me.

"Go on!" I say enthusiastically. It's important for me to establish that even though I agreed to go out with Short, I have no interest in what he does with his time. If I did care, then I would know that there was something wrong with me that stretched beyond lonely and desperate, which indeed would be truly frightening. "I'll get your check." I get the tab from a scowling Howard and check back once with Tully to make sure he doesn't need anything else.

"The boys are leaving," I say. Tully and I watch them help the girls with their coats. One of the girls drops a glove, and Short picks it up, hands it to her. He looks in our direction and gives a little wave to us. Then he says something to the girl. She stares at Tully and me, and then they both start laughing. I'm glad I can't hear what they are saying.

"That's nice," he says. "It's good for the young people to have a good time." We watch them go down the winding staircase, like Tully and I are parents watching our kids going off somewhere. I light another cigarette. I don't want to feel like a parent. My legs hurt and my back hurts.

Suddenly I spot Troy coming up the staircase. I rush over to him.

"All my customers are gone," I say. "Can I leave now?"

"Okay, love," he says. "Just make sure Christie knows so she can cover the area now.

Christie doesn't mind staying. She is having a great night, plus, she says, she's going out after work—with Troy.

"Troy?" I ask, making sure I heard correctly. Julie shrugs her shoulders and rolls her eyes.

"Why not?" she answers casually, picking up empty glasses from a table.

I pick up the credit card receipt signed by Short, on which I have received a healthy tip, compliments of the office, maybe even enough to take a cab home. I have to give Howard a percentage of my tips, but I think I'll lie and tell him that I made more than I did, so he'll have something extra to take home. I tell Tully it's time for me to go home. "I was thinking of going downstairs to play a game of pool," he says. "Are you up for a game?" It's 2:30 AM. I am tired, and I want to go home. I feel like I should stay, just for one game, but I am so tired. Aurora is probably hungry. And it is just so rare that I can leave this early.

"Nah, I've got to get some sleep," I say, not really looking at him. I can't look at him because I feel small for agreeing to go out with Short. I feel small for going home and going to sleep rather than spending a few extra minutes with someone who apparently has no one. There are times that I wish I was a better person.

All of a sudden I have an impulse to do something very unexpected. Something that the cute peppy waitress could do naturally but is an awkward gesture for someone like me. I lean over and kiss Tully on the cheek.

"Good night," I say. "You get home safe now." He looks just as surprised as I am, and for a moment there is this uncomfortable space between us which makes me feel like I did the wrong thing as he looks straight at me with a glassy, shocked expression.

"Good night, Sweetheart," he says. I don't mind him calling me that because of the way his voice breaks. A little pause separates the words so I hear them clearly—sweet and heart. It makes me wonder, as I walk down the winding stairs out of the dark castle and into the brightness of the street lamps, if maybe some small part of my heart is sweet, after all.

THE GUY WHO THOUGHT HE KNEW ME

M.O. Walsh

This guy had a brick for a face and no shoes on his feet. He sat there next to me and laid out his life like he was talking about somebody else, you know how people do.

So, *who* is Nelson Diaz? he said. A spic? Born to two white parents in the aisle of a subway train? Maybe. Maybe not. But we *do* know this: Nelson Diaz is a man who, at thirteen, decided to take everything literally. I mean *everything.*

But don't worry, he told me, these weren't lingo things like, "Give me a break" or "I'm freezing to death." No, Nelson Diaz wasn't a moron. He had never been that. If he had been anything, it was slender and lean and any other thing that makes old guys go gay. He was tall, muscled, hung. Whatever you wanted him to be.

Now, this guy is acting like we are old friends so I say, *Who are you again*? But that is just what he is trying to tell me. And the whole time I am just wanting to make eye contact with Sissy the bartender. She is my ex-wife, and it's like pulling teeth to get a drink from her now.

So, the type of things, him talking here, that young Diaz concerned himself with were things like following orders, tying knots, and paying the asking price. Things his mother taught him. This worked well for most of his years. He made top grades in school, and he even had some girlfriends, despite, what he called, *numerous* misunderstandings with women. And Nelson Diaz even got married, if you can believe it, to the second ugliest girl at Poloma High, and they had sex with no toys but just them for twenty years, with three children thanks to it. And Nelson can even show you the scar that showed up on his chest from the moment she died in the car with their kids.

But this, he assures me, is not meant to suggest that Nelson Diaz now leads a boring life. No, this is not meant for pity. In fact, Nelson Diaz is a scratch golfer who trades stocks online after midnight, because that is when he can be the most naked he can be.

The *real* problem for Nelson Diaz was that his mother, whose father was from Mexico, but was whiter than new socks, was a pragmatist. She told him that brushing his teeth in lines instead of in circles would lead most certainly to death. And that food fresh out of the microwave was no better than nuclear waste. And she believed that everything said was like water for the thirsty.

In fact, she once told young Nelson Diaz that being a widow was more like a window because people can see through to your pain. But, until his own wife died, Nelson had always thought she meant *pane*. So, do you see why it can be hard for Nelson?

Obviously, this is me talking now, I hadn't ever seen the toyless sex he claimed to have, or the children it produced, nor did I know if his mother was really a widow. And I didn't even want to think about him naked at midnight, clicking the mouse with his yoo-hoo. But still, these are the things that Nelson Diaz told me, when all I wanted was a drink from my Sissy because it's like the ice doesn't melt when she makes them.

And this guy Nelson Diaz is still wet from jogging, I'm guessing, and he keeps kneading his thigh with his thumbs. Then, right after he orders some cauliflower with cheese sauce (seriously) from Sissy, he confesses to never letting his gas tank drop below the halfway point. He *just can't do it*, he says. And then he repeats it. He also confesses to believing that beaches are made of dinosaur bones, crushed into sand over time. It is better, he said, if you think about it like that.

And Nelson Diaz is sitting *really* close to me now, and all he has on is this tank top with some pink running shorts that outline his genitals and are shameless, really. He needs some peanuts, he says. They give him energy. So he leans all over and looks behind the bar. He's got scratches on his feet and, like I said earlier, this big kind of block-looking face.

Because you see, him talking now, Nelson Diaz had a father who loved money more than anything. He'd pet his money and kiss its four corners. Then he would stack it up, tie it with rubber bands, and bury it under the house. That's what Nelson's mother told him, anyway. It was *better*, she said, to think of dead fathers that way.

So, how can you blame Nelson for hating the man? How can you blame kids for anything? Because it is easy to get confused, when you turn thirteen in such a dramatic way. And so now, Nelson doesn't know if he should go back and dig up under the house or what. Is there money under there or nothing? Is there anything to ever be gained?

I watched Nelson put his hands on the bar. The heat from them made the wood foggy, and I felt for him at that moment. I felt for this Nelson Diaz sitting next to me. Because, when Sissy came back, it had been at least ten minutes since he ordered. And I knew what Sissy would say, because I could see it all over her face that she didn't like this guy.

She was going to tell Nelson Diaz that *not only* did they not have peanuts, but they didn't have cauliflower with cheese sauce either. And, *not only* that, but they didn't serve food at all because as she had *just* remembered, they didn't even have a kitchen.

And I was really into Nelson's mind right then, because when Sissy told that she acted like it was normal for a person to forget about having something big like a kitchen. To forget about something that you either walk through or you don't, each and every day.

And I've always hated how Sissy bent the rules of everything. So, I tried not to watch her but I failed. She wiped down the beer taps like she didn't have a care. Then she raised her eyebrow at the Diaz guy who was just sitting there next to me, not hurting a thing.

"So, what do you *want?*" she asked him.

Nelson Diaz was confused, I'm sure, because he saw the way that she hated him for no reason. And he could feel, just like I can, the way that every thought in that woman's head is as pointed and sharp as a saw blade.

And I should have told Sissy to leave him alone right then because, after all, I was still there. But I am starting to think that doesn't really matter to her, that she can chew me all day and never get full. So, instead of saying anything to her, I grabbed Nelson by the back of his head and slammed his face against the bar.

Everyone looked at me, and Diaz slid right off of the stool. And when he jumped back up, he stuck his hands out in front of him. He looked around the room. I thought maybe he played the piano or something, I mean, his hands were really out there. Sissy threw a napkin at him because his head was bleeding. Then she turned back around, but not before glaring at *me*, and started checking the bottles for empties.

And then, Nelson Diaz, the guy who thought he knew me, kept his hands out in front of him the whole time, as he tiptoed, backwards, right out of that door he shouldn't have opened.

AUTHOR BIOGRAPHIES

Lee K. Abbott is the author of seven collections of short stories, most recently *All Things, All at Once: New & Selected Stories* (W. W. Norton). His many stories and reviews, as well as articles on American Literature have appeared in *The Atlantic, Harper's, The Georgia Review, The Gettysburg Review,* and nearly eighty other periodicals. It had been reprinted in *The Best American Short Stories, the Prize Stories: The O'Henry Awards,* and the *Pushcart Prize* volumes. He teaches in the MFA Program at The Ohio State University in Columbus.

Harlyn Aizley is a graduate of Brandeis and Harvard Universities. Her writing has appeared in national journals, magazines, and anthologies, and has aired on public radio stations nationwide. Hailed by *Publisher's Weekly* "as addictive as a good soap," Harlyn's memoir, *Buying Dad: One Woman's Search for the Perfect Sperm Donor* (Alyson), appeared on nonfiction bestseller lists nationwide as well as on the NPR Summer Reading List for 2003. Her second book, *Confessions of the Other Mother* (Beacon) is a 2007 Lambda Literary Award finalist. www.harlynaizley.com

Lee Capps grew up in Black Mountain, North Carolina and holds degrees from Duke, North Carolina State University, and Virginia Commonwealth University. He now lives with his wife and two young sons near Richmond, Virginia, where he works as a computer systems administrator. In 2002 he won the Fiction Fellowship of the College of Arts and Sciences at Virginia Commonwealth University. Recently his short fiction has appeared in *Ellery Queen's Mystery Magazine.* He is at work on a novel about family, belief, *and* outsider art. http://marge.homeunix.org/weblog

Karl Elder's "Pals" is from his novel-in-manuscript *Run*, partially funded by the Illinois Arts Council. He has other fictions in *Carriage House Review, Icon*, and the e-zine *Triptych.* More recently, his eighth collection of verse, *Gilgamesh at the Bellagio*, won publication in The National Poetry Review Award Book Series. Among Elder's honors are a Pulitzer Prize nomination; a Pushcart Prize; two appearances in The Best American Poetry; and the Chad Walsh, Lorine Niedecker, and Lucien Stryk Awards. For many years and since its inception, Elder has been linked with the literary magazine *Seems*—originally as a contributor, then poetry editor, and, since 1977, editor and publisher. A member of the National Eagle Scout Association and a Vigil Honor member of the Order of the Arrow, Elder is active in Scouting, for which his sons, Seth and Wade, serve as executives in the organization. www.karlelder.com

Lou Fisher is a recipient of the New Letters Literary Award for fiction. His stories have also appeared in two prize issues of *Mississippi Review* and in *Other Voices, The Crescent Review, The Florida Review, Bridge*, and many other journals, magazines, and anthologies. His earlier genre novel, *The Blue Ice Pilot*, was published by Warner Books and is still available from online book sites. Lou lives with his wife in downstate New York, a rural, nicely wooded area, but with plenty of bars. If he were to hang out in one of those bars, he would favor scotch, pool tables, red-haired ladies (like his wife), and country music. But he plays tennis instead. And he's learning to play the piano. All that after several years of teaching fiction and nonfiction for The Long Ridge Writers Group.

Robert Flanagan was born in Toledo, Ohio, and he is the author of the Marine Corps novel *Maggot* (Warner Books), and short story collections *Naked to Naked Goes* (Scribner) and *Loving Power* (Bottom Dog). He worked as a dishwasher, night watchman, and janitor before serving in the Marine Corps Reserve and going to the University of Toledo and University of Chicago. The cruel and beautiful sport of boxing has been his long-time addiction. Taught the rudiments of the sport by his father, an ex-marine combat vet and amateur southpaw lightweight, he sparred as a middleweight at the Y in Toledo and boxed in platoon bouts in the Corps. Recently retired from Ohio Wesleyan University where he was Professor of English and director of creative writing, Flanagan is at work on a boxing novel, *Champions*, from which "Fight Night" is taken. He lives in Delaware, Ohio with his wife Katy. www.robertflanagan.com

Mark Higgins, former bartender, now teaches creative writing and composition at Santa Ana College. His stories have been published in the *Paterson Literary Review, The Southern California Anthology, Slices of Orange, Journal 500, Benecia Bay Review, Suisun Valley Review, Aethlon: The Journal of Sport Literature*, and elsewhere. He lives in Irvine, California, with his wife and two children. His favorite pet—creature of the soulful eyes and mournful bark—is not a seal but a dog.

Molly Hoekstra is the author of *Upstream* (2001), a young adult novel and editor of *Am I Teaching Yet? Stories from the Teacher-Training Trenches* (2002).She has been a fellow at the Mary Anderson Center for the Arts and the Virginia Center for the Creative Arts. She lives in Nashville with her husband, singer-songwriter Doug Hoekstra and their son, Jude. She is currently working on a second YA novel. www.myspace.com/amiteachingyet

Matt Oliver never finished high school, but got his GED in 1981 and enlisted in the Navy in 1982. After discharge from the Navy in 1986, Matt remained in San Diego rather than returning to the San Francisco Bay Area where he was born and raised. He then moved to Colorado in 1988 where he worked on a ranch and to Ohio in 1990 to work on a farm. He met his wife Lynn in Ohio, and they moved to Norfolk, VA after they married in 1991. His son Bryan was born in 1993, and that inspired Matt to return to school where he completed a BA in English and an MFA in Creative Writing. His daughter Laurie was born in 1995. He now teaches English at Old Dominion University in Norfolk.

Michael Piafsky is currently an Assistant Professor at Spring Hill College. He received his PhD from The University of Missouri-Columbia and his Master's degree from The Writing Seminars at Johns Hopkins University. Michael also worked in advertising and served as an editor on *The Missouri Review*. He currently lives in Mobile, AL with his wife and two children.

Bruce Taylor, author of *Pity the World: Poems Selected and New* (2005) Plain View Press, has had his poetry, fiction, and translations appear in such places as *Carve, The Chicago Review, The Exquisite Corpse, Light, The Nation, Nerve, The New York Quarterly, Poetry, Unlikely Stories, Vestal Review* and *E2ink-1: the Best of the Online Journals*. Taylor has won awards and fellowships from the Bush Artist Foundation, the Council of Wisconsin Writers, the Wisconsin Arts Board, the NEA, NEH, and Fulbright-Hayes. He is the recipient of the 2004 Award for Excellence in Scholarship from the University Of Wisconsin Eau Claire where he teaches in the Department of English. One of his current projects is a short fiction series called "Story Is..." of which this selection is a part. http://www.uwec.edu/taylorb/

M.O. Walsh was born and raised in Baton Rouge, LA. His work has appeared in *Epoch, Greensboro Review*, and *New Delta Review*, among others, and has been anthologized in *Best New American Voices, Stories from the Blue Moon Cafe, French Quarter Fiction*, and *Louisiana in Words*. He currently lives and writes in Oxford, MS, with his wife Sarah and dog Gus.

G. K. Wuori is the author of over sixty stories published throughout the world in the U.S., Japan, India, Germany, Spain, Algeria, Ireland, and Brazil. A Pushcart Prize winner and recipient of an Illinois Arts Council Fellowship, his work has appeared in such journals as *The Gettysburg Review, The Missouri Review, The Barcelona Review, The Massachusetts Review*, and *Five Points*. Stories recently published or forthcoming can be seen in

StoryQuarterly, Shenandoah, and *TriQuarterly.*
His collection, *Nude in Tub,* was a New Voices
Award Nominee by the Quality Paperback
Book Club and his novel, *An American
Outrage,* was *Foreword Magazine's* Book of the
Year in fiction. He currently lives in
Sycamore, Illinois where he writes a column
called Cold Iron at www.gkwuori.com.
www.gkwuori.com

Gary Young is a poet and artist whose honors
include grants from the National Endowment
for the Humanities, the Vogelstein
Foundation, the California Arts Council, and
two fellowship grants from the National
Endowment for the Arts. He has received a
Pushcart Prize, and his book of poems, *The
Dream of a Moral Life,* won the James D.
Phelan Award. He is the author of several
other collections of poetry including *Hands,
Days, Braver Deeds,* which won the Peregrine
Smith Poetry Prize, *No Other Life,* winner of
the William Carlos Williams Award of the
Poetry Society of America, and most
recently, *Pleasure.* He is the co-editor of *The
Geography of Home: California's Poetry of
Place,* and has produced a series of artist's
books, most notably *Nine Days: New York, A
Throw of the Dice* and *My Place Here Below.*
Since 1975 he has designed, illustrated, and
printed limited edition books and broadsides
at his Greenhouse Review Press. His print
work is represented in numerous collections
including the Museum of Modern Art, the
Victoria and Albert Museum, The Getty
Center for the Arts, and special collection
libraries throughout the country. He lives
in the mountains north of Santa Cruz,
California with his wife and two sons.
www.gary-young.org

Visit
www.barstoryblog.com
www.nanbyrne.com
Order Online

Books may be ordered direct or through
Small Press Distribution at SPDBooks.org
or Baker& Taylor Books

Bottom Dog Press

d.a.levy & the mimeograph revolution
eds. Ingrid Swanberg & Larry Smith
1-933964-07-3 276 pgs. & dvd $25

Evensong: Contemporary American Poets on Spirituality
eds. Gerry LaFemina & Chad Prevost
ISBN 1-933964-01-4 276 pgs. $18

120 Charles Street, The Village:
Journals & Other Writings 1949-1950 by Holly Beye
0-933087-99-3 240 pgs. $15.00

The Search for the Reason Why:
New and Selected Poems by Tom Kryss
0-933087-96-9 192 pgs. $14.00

Family Matters: Poems of Our Families
eds. Ann Smith and Larry Smith
0-933087-95-0 230 pgs. $16.00

America Zen: A Gathering of Poets
eds. Ray McNiece and Larry Smith
0-933087-91-8 224 pgs. $15.00

O Taste and See: Food Poems
eds. by David Lee Garrison & Terry Hermsen
0-933087-82-9 198 pgs. $14.00

Songs of the Woodcutter:
Zen Poems of Wang Wei and Taigu Ryokan
by Larry Smith & Monte Page
0-933087-80-2 (CD & Booklet) $12.00

Bottom Dog Press
PO Box 425 / Huron, OH 44839
Homepage for Ordering:
http://members.aol.com/Lsmithdog/bottomdog
Include $2.00 with any order for shipping.

BIRD DOG

PUBLISHING

Winter Apples: Poems by Paul S. Piper
978-1-933964-08-9 88 pgs. $14.00

Lake Effect: Poems by Laura Treacy Bentley
1-933964-05-7 108 pgs. $14.00

Faces and Voices: Tales by Larry Smith
1-933964-04-9 136 pgs. $14.00

Depression Days on an Appalachian Farm: Poems
by Robert L. Tener
1-933964-03-0 80 pgs. $14.00

*120 Charles Street, The Village:
Journals & Other Writings 1949-1950* by Holly Beye
0-933087-99-3 240 pgs. $15.00

http://members.aol.com/lsmithdog/bottomdog/BirdDogPage.html

Printed in the United States
81877LV00001B/85-132